KATHIE DeNOSKY

Betrothed for the Baby

D0011569

Silhouette®

Desire

Published by Silhouette Books
America's Publisher of Contemporary Romance

SILHOUETTE BOOKS

ISBN 0-373-76712-9

BETROTHED FOR THE BABY

Visit Silhouette Books at www.eHarlequin.com

Printed in U.S.A.

Books by Kathie DeNosky

Silhouette Desire

Did You Say Married?! #1296
The Rough And Ready Rancher #1355
His Baby Surprise #1374
Maternally Yours #1418
Cassie's Cowboy Daddy #1439
Cowboy Boss #1457
A Lawman in Her Stocking #1475
In Bed with the Enemy #1521
Lonetree Ranchers: Brant #1528
Lonetree Ranchers: Morgan #1540
Lonetree Ranchers: Colt #1551
Remembering One Wild Night #1559
Baby at His Convenience #1595
A Rare Sensation #1633
*Engagement between Enemies #1700
*Reunion of Revenge #1707
*Betrothed for the Baby #1712

Silhouette Books

Home for the Holidays
"New Year's Baby"

Signature Select

Taken by Storm
"Whirlwind"

*The Illegitimate Heirs

KATHIE DeNOSKY

lives in her native southern Illinois with her husband and one very spoiled Jack Russell terrier. She writes highly sensual stories with a generous amount of humor. Kathie's books have appeared on the Waldenbooks bestseller list and received the Write Touch Readers' Award from WisRWA and the National Readers' Choice Award. Kathie enjoys going to rodeos, traveling to research settings for her books and listening to country music. Readers may contact Kathie at: P.O. Box 2064, Herrin, Illinois 62948-5264 or e-mail her at kathie@kathiedenosky.com.

This book is dedicated to my editor, Tina Colombo. Thank you for your unwavering support and encouragement. You're the very best.

And a special thank-you to my son, Bryan, for his help with the Spanish in this book.

Te amo, mi hijo.

One

When Hunter O'Banyon glanced over at the pretty little blonde he'd met only moments ago, adrenaline began to pump through his veins. Her porcelain cheeks were flushed with a mixture of heat and excitement, and he could tell from the sparkle of urgency in her violet eyes that he was in for one hell of a ride.

"I hope you don't mind, but this is going to have to be faster than I'd planned," she said, sounding a little breathless.

Grinning, he nodded. "Bring it on. I can take it as fast as you want to go."

"I like the way you think." Her smile caused his

heart to race like a twelve-stroke engine hitting on all cylinders. "Hang on, big guy. This might get a little wild."

Hunter took a deep breath and braced himself. "Burn it, darlin'."

At the same time as she pushed the gas pedal all the way to the floor, she reached out to flip a switch on the dash. Lights and the keening wail of a siren competed with the sound of spinning tires kicking up a huge cloud of gravel and southwest Texas dust as the pickup truck careened away from the tarmac at Devil's Fork Community Airfield.

When Hunter had discovered there was no commercial air service to the little town, he'd wondered why the pilot of the Cessna Skyhawk he'd chartered to fly him to Devil's Fork from El Paso had laughed like a hyena when Hunter had called it an airport. Now he knew why. The entire thing consisted of an asphalt landing strip that he'd bet barely met FAA standards, a storage shed that leaned precariously to one side and a wooden pole with a tattered wind sock attached to the top just above the United States and Texas flags. As far as he could tell, there weren't even any lights for landing at night. He could only hope the Life Medevac operation looked better.

"By the way, I'm Callie Marshall, the flight nurse on the Evac II team," the blonde said conversationally.

Nice name for a nice-looking woman, he thought

as they approached the edge of town. "I'm Hunter O'Banyon."

"Thank God." She grinned. "When my pager went off, I didn't give you time to introduce yourself, and it suddenly occurred to me that you might not be the man I was supposed to meet."

His heart stalled and he had to clear his suddenly dry throat. When she smiled, Callie Marshall wasn't just pretty, she was drop-dead gorgeous.

"What were the chances of anyone else flying into Devil's Fork?" he asked when he finally got his vocal cords to work.

Her delightful laughter was one of the nicest sounds he'd heard in a long time. "Good point," she said, nodding. "I think you're the first person I've heard of flying into Devil's Fork since I arrived two months ago."

"Somehow that doesn't surprise me." He tightened his safety harness when she turned a corner, seemingly on two wheels. "Did you arrive by plane?"

"No way." She shook her head, causing her ponytail to sway back and forth. "I drove over from Houston. I wasn't about to take one of those puddle-jumper flights in here."

As they sped down Main Street, Hunter decided that if he'd blinked, he might have missed the entire town. Besides the fact that Callie was going so fast it wasn't much more than a blur, the business district was only a few blocks long and there wasn't much more than two or three blocks to the residential section.

"Mary Lou, our dispatcher, said you're from the Miami area. It might take a while for you to get used to Devil's Fork. It's about six hundred miles from the nearest beach and not exactly a hotbed of social activity."

"No kidding." He cringed when they sailed through a four-way stop on the opposite end of town without so much as slowing down. "I knew this place was small, but I expected something a little bigger than this."

"I did, too," she agreed. "After I drove through it the first time, I had a hard time believing there was enough of a call for a medevac operation to be based here. But I was wrong."

Hunter thought back to what he'd read in the file he'd been handed on the business his grandmother had given him to run. "The way I understand it, we're the only emergency service available for sections of five different counties."

She nodded. "The population is so sparse in this part of Texas, it isn't cost-effective for communities to have their own ambulance." Shrugging, she steered the truck onto a dirt-packed road leading up to a large aircraft hangar with Life Medevac Helicopter Service painted on the side. "Besides, if they had a ground unit, it would take too long to reach most of the people and even longer to get them to a hospital. We're their best hope for emergency medical care."

When she drove the truck around the side of the building, Hunter breathed a little easier. The Life Medevac base appeared to be in much better condition than the Devil's Fork airfield. Besides the well-kept hangar, there were two brand-new, top-of-the-line Bell EMS helicopters sitting on brightly painted helipads, and the entire area was ringed with what looked to be state-of-the-art lighting for night takeoffs and landings.

"I'll see you when we get back," she said, jamming the gearshift into Park at the same time she killed the engine and threw open the driver's door. "I have a flight to catch."

"Thanks for the ride," Hunter called, getting out of the truck.

Turning, she gave him another one of her killer smiles. "I almost forgot to tell you—beware of Mary Lou's coffee. She'll tell you it's the best you've ever had, but don't believe it." She grimaced. "It's awful."

As he stood there staring at Callie slowly jogging toward the waiting helicopter, he couldn't put his finger on what it was about her, but something bothered him. Aside from the fact that she'd driven the truck through town as though the hounds of hell were chasing them and she now moved as if she had all the time in the world, there was something about the snug way her navy-blue flight suit fit her around the middle that didn't seem quite right.

But when she disappeared inside the cabin space of the chopper and the door slid shut behind her, he quickly dismissed his concerns as Evac II lifted off the helipad. Although Emerald Larson had assured him that she'd seen to it that all the equipment was up-to-date and exceeded state requirements, he intended to order new flight suits in a color that could be more easily differentiated from other first responders that might be on scene when the Life Medevac crews arrived. And he'd make sure everyone wore the right size.

"You must be Hunter O'Banyon, the new boss of this outfit."

At the sound of the female voice behind him, Hunter turned to face a woman he'd judge to be somewhere in her late sixties or early seventies. With curly snow-white hair, a perfectly round face and a pair of narrow reading glasses perched on her nose, she looked as if she could easily play Mrs. Claus in a Christmas pageant.

He smiled as he extended his hand. "That would be me. And you must be Mary Lou Carson."

"The one and only." Grinning, she firmly shook his hand. "Come on in the dispatch room and rest a spell. I'll pour you a cup of the best coffee you've ever had, then I'll show you your quarters."

Reaching into the bed of the pickup truck, Hunter grabbed his luggage and followed Mary Lou out of the late-August heat and into the air-conditioned office of

Member Correspondence

RUSH DELIVERY!

BUSINESS REPLY MAIL

FIRST-CLASS MAIL   PERMIT NO. 2744   HOPKINS MN

POSTAGE WILL BE PAID BY ADDRESSEE

CREATIVE HOME ARTS CLUB
PO BOX 3472
MINNETONKA MN 55343-4858

CREATIVE HOME ARTS CLUB

JOIN or GIVE A GIFT!

1 year only $24 — Just $2 per month!

☐ **YES! I'm joining the Creative Home Arts Club** 07EAD41

Member No. ☐☐☐☐☐☐☐

Your Name _____

Address _____

City _____ State _____ Zip _____

Phone # _____ E-Mail _____

Allow 4-6 weeks for delivery of membership materials. For Canadian memberships, please send $36 in Canadian funds (includes 6% GST) for annual dues [CA70BI].
$20 of each year's dues is for *Today's Creative Home Arts* magazine.

☐ **YES! Please send a Gift Membership for the Creative Home Arts Club to:** GA74GG1

(Also, please complete section above for billing and so we can announce your gift.)

Name _____

Address _____

City _____ State _____ Zip _____

Phone # _____ E-Mail _____

☐ **BILL ME LATER**   ☐ **CHECK OR MONEY ORDER ENCLOSED ($24)**

Allow 4-6 weeks for delivery of membership materials. For Canadian memberships, please send $36 in Canadian funds (includes 6% GST) for annual dues [CA70BIG].
$20 of each year's dues is for *Today's Creative Home Arts* magazine.

EA741

AMIC0037

the hangar. When she led him into the dispatch room, he looked around at the framed military medals hanging on the wall beside the door.

"Did these belong to your husband?" he asked conversationally.

"Some of them." Mary Lou walked over to a small kitchen area on the opposite side of the room to stir the delicious-smelling contents of a huge pot on the electric range. "The rest are mine."

When she walked back over to where he stood, she handed him a cup of coffee, then motioned for him to sit in one of several chairs on the opposite side of a scarred wooden desk. "Take a load off, Hunter."

"What branch of the military were you in?" he asked, sitting down.

"Lester and I were both career Navy." She walked between the desk and a built-in counter filled with radio equipment, a computer and several telephones to settle herself into an old wooden desk chair that looked as if it might have been around since World War II. "He was an aircraft mechanic and I was a nurse. He died in an accident onboard an aircraft carrier not long before we were supposed to retire."

"I'm sorry." Hunter knew all too well what it was like to lose someone unexpectedly.

"Don't be sorry," she said, surprising him. "Lester died doing what he loved most—working on fighter jets. That's the best way any of us can hope to go out of this world." Before he could respond, she shrugged. "That's why I'm a dispatcher here. After my arthritis forced me to stop working the floor in a hospital, I took this job. When people call with an emergency, I sometimes stay on the line and talk them through whatever medical crisis they have until one of our crews arrives. It's almost as satisfying as nursing."

Hunter took a sip of coffee as he considered what Mary Lou said. But as the bitter taste spread over his tongue, he had to force himself to swallow. Quickly setting the cup on the desk, he barely controlled the urge to shudder. What Callie had told him about the coffee being awful had been an understatement. The stuff was as thick as syrup and tasted as though it had been made with quinine.

Coughing, he looked up to see Mary Lou watching him expectantly. He could tell she was waiting for him to tell her how good it was.

"You like your coffee strong, don't you?" he asked, trying not to grimace.

She shrugged. "I like my coffee to be just the way I like a man—strong and the best I've ever had."

If he'd thought her coffee was enough to send his system into shock, her outspokenness finished the job. He couldn't have been more dumbfounded if he'd tried. Unable to think of a thing to say, he waited to see what she'd say next. Unless he'd misjudged her, that shouldn't take very long.

Her knowing smile clued him in on the fact that she'd known her statement would render him speech-less. "There's a few things about me you might as well know up front, Hunt. I don't mince words. I say exactly what I think because I'm old enough to get away with it and I've never been one to beat around the bush."

"I can respect that." Hunter had no idea where Mary Lou was going with this, but he could tell she had more on her mind.

"I'm glad to hear you say that, because what I'm going to tell you now might not set real well."

"I'm listening."

"I'm going to treat you like I treat everyone else around here because I'm not impressed by much of anything anymore. And that includes you being Emerald Larson's grandson."

Hunter frowned. He'd specifically asked Emerald not to divulge his relationship to her. For one thing, he didn't need the added pressure of living up to someone's expectations. And for another, he still hadn't fully come to terms with being her grandson.

"How did you learn about—"

"Emerald and I go way back. She hasn't always been on the top of the heap. When she was a teenager, she worked behind the soda counter in my father's drugstore." Mary Lou grinned. "She was like an older sister to me, and we've stayed in touch over the years."

Hunter wasn't particularly happy about having one of Emerald's lifelong friends working for him. He didn't like the idea of not being able to make a move without his manipulative grandmother knowing about it.

"If you're worried about me running to Emerald to report everything you do, don't waste your time," Mary Lou said as though she'd read his mind. "I don't carry tales. If she wants to know what's going on with you, she'll have to ask you herself."

"That's good to hear." Whether he should or not, Hunter believed the woman.

Draining the last of her coffee, Mary Lou placed her cup on the desk and stood up. "Now that we have that out of the way, I'll show you to your living quarters and let you get settled in while I finish up the beef stew I put on for our supper." She pointed to his cup. "Would you like that warmed up?"

He quickly shook his head. "I'm not much of a coffee drinker." He didn't want to hurt her feelings, but if he never drank another drop of the bitter brew, it would be all too soon.

She shook her head. "I don't know what's wrong with you young people. I'm the only one working here who likes coffee."

As Hunter grabbed his suitcase and followed her through a doorway and down a hall toward the back of the hangar, he suspected the others' reluctance to drink Mary Lou's coffee had everything in the world to do with self-defense and nothing to do with not liking coffee.

"This is your office," she said, passing a door on the way to the back of the building. Pointing to a door across the hall, she added, "And this is the on-duty crew's sleeping quarters. We have three crews working rotating twenty-four-hour shifts—two days on duty and four off. Of course, on the outside chance that we get a call while one crew is out, the first two days that a crew is off duty, they're on call."

"What about you? What are your hours?"

"I'm here round the clock. When I'm not dispatching a crew, I'm cooking and handing out advice that nobody seems to listen to." She laughed as she pointed to a door next to the crew quarters. "This is my room. I have a ringer in here that wakes me up when we have a night call or I decide to take a nap."

Hunter frowned. "Who's the dispatcher on your days off?"

She continued walking toward a door at the end of the hall. "On the rare occasions that I take a day off, one of the members of the off-duty crew fills in for me."

"You don't have regularly scheduled time off?" He didn't like the sound of that. Aside from Emerald taking advantage of Mary Lou, he wasn't sure that it was even legal for the woman to be working that much.

"Don't get your shorts in a bunch, Hunter," Mary Lou said as if she'd read his mind. "I don't have family, and working here at Life Medevac is what makes me happy and keeps me going. I love what I do, so don't go getting any ideas about making me take time off on a regular basis, because I won't do it." She opened the door to his room, then, stepping back, pointed to his luggage. "Are all your things in that one suitcase?"

He nodded. "I stored the rest of my things until I find a place in Devil's Fork."

"Good idea." The woman nodded her approval. "Now go ahead and get your gear stowed away while I radio Evac II and find out the status of their patient and what time they estimate they'll get back to base."

Hunter stared after Mary Lou as she breezed out the door and down the hall as if her working without regular days off was a nonissue. But he wasn't so sure. It wasn't just a question of the labor laws. Her age and well-being had to be taken into consideration, as well. She might seem like a dynamo with boundless energy, but working 24-7 would be hard on a much younger person, let alone a woman close to seventy.

As he lifted his suitcase and placed it on the edge of the bed to unpack, he decided there were several things he needed to do right away. Not only did he need to order the correct size flight suits for everyone, he'd have to check into Texas labor laws.

Putting away the last of his clothes, he looked around. It was a good thing he always traveled light. The room was barely big enough for the twin bed, small chest of drawers and bedside table. There was no way he'd have had room for anything but his clothes.

But then, he didn't need a lot of room. For the past five years he hadn't cared how spacious his accommodations had been or even where they'd been located. After working construction so hard each day that he'd been too tired to think or remember, all he'd needed was a place to sleep, shower and change clothes. With any luck, there would be enough work to keep him just as busy at Life Medevac.

At the sound of a helicopter landing outside, he walked down the hall to the dispatch room. "They weren't gone long."

Mary Lou nodded. "Juanita Rodriguez thought she was going to have her baby, but it turned out to be false labor." Smiling, she added, "She's only nineteen and it's her first pregnancy. She and her husband, Miguel, are worried they won't make it to the hospital in time."

"I hear that's a big concern for most first-time parents." A twinge of regret ran through Hunter. Anticipating the arrival of a child was something he would never experience.

But he didn't have time to dwell on the disturbing thought as the flight crew from Evac II entered the dispatch room. Besides Callie, the crew consisted of a sandy-haired man who looked to be in his forties and a fresh-faced kid of about twenty.

"The name's George Smith," the man said, smiling

as he walked over to shake Hunter's hand. Almost as tall as Hunter's own six-foot-three-inch frame, George was built like a heavyweight prizefighter, and if his grip was any indication, as strong as one. "I'm the pilot for the Evac II team." He nodded toward the younger man. "And that kid over there is Corey Timmons, the EMT on our crew."

"It's nice to meet you, Mr. O'Banyon," Corey said, stepping forward to pump Hunter's hand enthusiastically. "We've been looking forward to you taking over."

"Call me Hunter." He wasn't surprised to hear the employees had been looking forward to a change in administration. From the file he'd been given, when Emerald bought Life Medevac, the employees hadn't been paid their wages in several weeks.

Grinning, the young man's brown eyes danced mischievously. "We're glad to see you survived the drive across town with Callie behind the wheel."

Hunter chuckled. "Was there doubt?"

"After flying into Devil's Fork with Crash Jenson at the controls of that little four-seater prop job, we kinda wondered if her driving wouldn't finish you off," George added, laughing.

"If you two keep joking about my driving, I'll stop making those chocolate-chip-oatmeal cookies you love so much," Callie warned good-naturedly as she crossed the room to the kitchen area, where Mary Lou was putting the finishing touches on the crew's dinner.

"We take it all back," Corey said earnestly as he walked over to grab a plate for Mary Lou to fill with a generous helping of stew.

"You bet," George said, nodding vigorously. "We were just joking around, Callie. Whatever you do, don't stop making those cookies." Turning to Hunter, he confided, "You've never tasted anything as good in your entire life as her chocolate-chip-oatmeal cookies."

"I'll look forward to trying them," Hunter said, enjoying the easy banter.

As George moved to get a plate of stew, Hunter watched Callie open the refrigerator to remove a carton of orange juice and once again noticed the way her flight suit fit. The navy-blue fabric was fairly loose everywhere but in her midsection and she looked as if…

A sudden cold feeling of intense dread began to fill Hunter's chest and he had to swallow hard against the bile rising in his throat. Callie Marshall wasn't just carrying a few extra pounds around the middle. She was several months pregnant.

Two

As she walked past Hunter to sit down in one of the chairs in front of Mary Lou's desk, Callie wondered what on earth she'd done to come under such close scrutiny. His intense stare had followed her from the moment she'd walked into the room and caused her skin to tingle as if he'd reached out and touched her.

Shaking her head to clear it, she decided her uncharacteristic reaction to him had to be because her hormones were all out of whack due to her pregnancy. It was the only reasonable explanation she could think of to explain it.

His concentrated stare had probably been nothing

more than the result of noticing her thickening midsection. He was no doubt trying to figure out whether she was just a bit plump or expecting a baby.

Careful to keep her voice low to avoid calling the others' attention to the fact that she'd caught him staring, she smiled as she turned to meet his intense green gaze. "In case you're wondering about my odd shape, I'm four and a half months pregnant."

Running an agitated hand through his dark brown hair, he looked a little uncomfortable. "I...didn't mean to—"

"Don't worry about it." She smiled, hoping to put him at ease. "It's not like it's a big secret. And, as you can see, I'm certainly not trying to hide my pregnancy."

"Your husband is okay with you flying while you're pregnant?" He shook his head. "I'm sorry. It's none of my business."

It was an odd question, but the concern on his handsome face and in his deep voice was genuine. "Don't worry about it. I don't have a husband, so it's a nonissue." She shrugged. "I'm unmarried, uncommitted and quite content to stay that way."

"I didn't mean to pry." He looked more uncomfortable than before.

"It's not a problem. I'm actually looking forward to single motherhood."

He looked as if he intended to say something, but Corey chose that moment to walk over and plop down in the chair beside her. "Have we sucked up enough to get more cookies or do we need to grovel a little more?"

Callie laughed at the likable young EMT. "No, I think you've redeemed yourself enough for another batch of chocolate-chip-oatmeal cookies."

"If you'll excuse me, I think I'll go check out my office," Hunter said suddenly, turning to walk down the hall.

Staring after her new boss, she wondered what had caused his abrupt change. When she'd met him at the airfield, he'd been congenial and outgoing. But within the span of a few minutes his mood had become pensive and troubled. Was he concerned that she would be unable to do her job?

She rose to her feet to follow him into the office and reassure him that she was perfectly capable of carrying out her duties, but the dispatch radio chose that moment to crackle to life.

"Looks like we have another run," Mary Lou said, crossing the room to answer the call.

As Callie listened to the highway patrol officer relay the location of the one-car accident on Interstate 10 and the patrolman's assessment of the driver's injuries, she, George and Corey started for the door. "Tell him we're on the way."

"ETA is fifteen minutes," George said.

"Keep the stew warm," Corey added.

Out of the corner of her eye Callie saw Hunter

reenter the room. His concerned expression reinforced her determination to set his mind at ease. But their talk would have ·to wait until later. Whether or not he believed she was capable of doing her job, she had an accident victim depending on her for emergency medical attention. And she wasn't about to let her patient down.

Drenched in a cold sweat, Hunter awoke with a jerk and, swinging his legs over the side of the bed, sat up. Propping his elbows on his knees, he cradled his head in his hands as he tried to chase away the remnants of his nightmare.

He hadn't dreamed about the accident in almost six months. But it was just as real now as it had been when he'd lived through it five years ago. He and his fiancée, Ellen Reichert, a second-year resident at the Mount Sinai Medical Center in Miami, had flown into Central America to deliver medical supplies and administer first aid to some of the remote villages hit the hardest by a category-four hurricane. Everything about the trip had been routine and uneventful until he'd circled the landing site for their last stop. That's when all hell had broken loose and the course of his life had changed forever.

The twin-turbine helicopter he'd been piloting had suddenly lost oil pressure, then, before he could get it safely set down, it stalled out. He didn't remember a lot of the details of what happened after that, only that he'd fought the controls with little success. The chopper had ended up tilting precariously in midair, then come down hard on its starboard side.

His first thought had been to make sure that Ellen was all right, then get them out of what was left of the helicopter. But the blood in his veins had turned to ice when he'd called her name and she'd failed to respond. He'd placed his fingers to the side of her neck and, detecting a faint pulse, scrambled to release their seat belts. Pushing the door on the port side of the chopper open, he'd carefully lifted her up through the opening, then carried her a safe distance from the wreckage.

When she'd regained consciousness, they'd both known she didn't have long, and that's when his devastating heartbreak had turned to total despair. She'd told him that she'd been waiting for the perfect time to tell him she'd recently learned she was pregnant. With her dying breath she'd told him how much she loved him and how sorry she was that she had to go, then, closing her eyes, she'd quietly slipped away.

The ensuing investigation into the crash had proven the accident had been caused by mechanical failure and there was nothing he could have done to prevent it. But he'd quit flying that day and struggled for the past five years, feeling guilty because he'd walked away with nothing more than cuts and bruises, blaming himself for living when the woman he'd loved and their future child had died. He'd spent countless hours going over every detail of the accident, wondering if there was something he could have done differently, something that could have lessened her injuries or saved her life. But try as he might, he couldn't think of anything that would have changed the outcome.

He took a deep shuddering breath and tried to relegate the disturbing memories to the back of his mind. There was no doubt why the horrific dream had returned, and he couldn't say he was overly surprised that it had. After discovering that Callie was pregnant, all he'd been able to think about was once again being responsible for the lives of a woman and her unborn child. Even though she wasn't on his flight crew, as her employer it was ultimately his job to see to her safety.

Fortunately her shift had ended right after the Evac II team had returned from transporting the car accident victim to a hospital in El Paso. That meant that he had four days to come up with a convincing argument to get her to ground herself. And unless her crew was called out as backup for Evac III, she and her baby would be safe.

Now all Hunter had to do was figure out a way to keep them that way.

"Give me a second," Callie called when it sounded as if whoever was at her front door would knock it off its hinges with their insistent pounding. Wiping the flour from her hands with her apron, she turned her CD player down and hurried from the kitchen to open the door. "What's so important that—"

She stopped short at the sight of Hunter O'Banyon standing on her tiny front porch. Lord have mercy, but he was one of the best looking men she'd ever seen. He was dressed in a black T-shirt and worn blue jeans. The soft fabrics fit him like a second skin and emphasized the width of his broad shoulders and his narrow hips. When she glanced at his arms, the sight of his bulging biceps stretching the knit sleeves of his shirt sent a shiver of awareness straight up her spine.

Callie gave herself a mental shake. What on earth was wrong with her? And why in the name of heaven was she ogling the man as if he were a fudge-nut brownie with rich chocolate frosting?

"Are you all right?" His expression was one of deep concern.

"Of—" she swallowed hard "—course. Why wouldn't I be?" Other than being embarrassed that her hair was piled on her head in total disarray, her shorts and T-shirt were the oldest things she had in her closet and she was coated with a fine dusting of flour, she was just peachy.

"I knocked for five minutes before you answered the door. I thought something might be wrong." He rubbed his hand over the back of his neck. "Never mind. Do you have a few minutes? We need to talk."

What could he possibly think they needed to discuss? And why did he have to show up after she'd received a phone call from her mother?

At least once a week since telling her mother she was pregnant they'd gone through the same old routine of her mother wanting to know who the father of Callie's baby was and why she was so insistent on keeping the man's identity a secret. Frustrated beyond words with her mother's persistence, by the time Callie had ended the phone call, she'd already measured the ingredients for several dozen sugar cookies and had pulled the box of oats from the cupboard for a double batch of chocolate-chip-oat-meal cookies.

Some women cleaned house when they were upset. Callie baked.

"Do you mind if I come in?" Hunter asked, returning her to the present.

"I'm sorry. Please come in." She stepped back for him to enter her small cottage. "I was just baking some—oh no! My cookies!" Remembering the peanut butter cookies she'd put into the oven just before hearing him pound on the door, she made a beeline for the kitchen with him hot on her heels.

"Damn! When you make cookies, you don't fool around, do you?" he said, looking around.

Taking the baking sheet from the oven, she placed it on the top of the stove, then glanced at the table and countertops. Plates of cookies covered every available surface.

Shaking her head at the sight, she nibbled on her lower lip. She must have been more upset over her mother's phone call than she'd realized.

"Would you like some milk and cookies?" She grinned. "I have plenty."

"No kidding." His deep chuckle caused a wave of goose bumps to sweep over her skin. "What are you going to do with all of them?"

"They won't last long around George and Corey."

She opened a cabinet to get something to store the cookies in, but the feel of Hunter's broad chest pressed to her side as he stepped forward to reach for several of the plastic containers on the top shelf sent a charge of excitement skipping over every nerve in her body. When he handed them to her, then stepped back, she had trouble drawing her next breath.

Unnerved, her hand trembled as she took the containers from him. "Th-thank you."

He gave her a short nod, then moved farther away. "I think I will take you up on that offer of some milk and cookies."

Pouring them each a glass of milk, she set one at the far end of the table and started to sit down at the opposite end. Hunter was immediately behind her, holding the chair, and his close proximity unsettled her so much that she almost turned over her glass.

What in blazes was wrong with her? She not only felt as jumpy as a frightened rabbit, she'd suddenly turned into a major klutz.

When he sat down across from her, he studied the plates of cookies between them. "What do you suggest I start with first?"

"I like the oatmeal cookies, but that's probably because I use chocolate chips instead of raisins," she said, reaching for one of the tasty treats.

He nodded as he took a cookie from one of the plates. "I'm kind of partial to peanut butter myself." Taking a bite, his eyes widened. "Corey and George weren't exaggerating—these are some of the best cookies I've ever tasted."

As they munched on the cookies, Callie wondered what it was he thought they needed to discuss. For the life of her she couldn't think of anything so important that he'd pay her a visit on her day off.

"What did you want to talk to me about?" she asked, hoping the sooner he stated the purpose for his visit, the sooner he'd leave. She desperately needed to regain her composure.

Taking a deep breath, he set his empty glass on the table, then caught her gaze with his. "I'm concerned that your job might be a little too much for a woman in your condition."

She laughed. "Contrary to what you might think, pregnancy is not a disability."

"I understand that," he said, nodding. "But at times I'm sure it's extremely tiring."

"I'm not going to pretend that it isn't." She rose to place their glasses in the dishwasher, then started stacking cookies in the containers for freezing. "But there are also times when we'll go for a day or two without an emergency call and I'm exhausted from sheer boredom. Besides, my obstetrician doesn't have a problem with me working as a flight nurse, so if you're worried that it's too strenuous for me, don't. Corey and George are both very conscientious and won't let me do any heavy lifting. And when we're not out on calls, I make sure to take regular naps."

"Yes, but there's other things to be considered, such as turbulence or pilot error," he said as he handed her plates full of cookies to be stored in the plasticware.

"I trust George. He's a good pilot."

"I'm not saying he isn't."

She snapped the lid shut on the box, then started filling another one. "What *are* you saying?"

He rubbed the back of his neck as if to relieve tension. "Aren't you worried about having to make a rough landing or a possible crash?"

"Not really." She couldn't for the life of her figure out why he was so overly concerned. Every pilot she'd ever known considered flying the safest mode of transportation. "In the event that something like that happens, I'm in no greater danger because I'm pregnant than I would be if I wasn't."

"But—"

"I see no reason why you're so worried about it, but if you think it's that important, why don't you review the employment records and put me on the crew with the best pilot?"

To her surprise, he placed his large hands on her shoulders and turned her to face him. But instead of arguing his point further, he stared at her for several long seconds before he muttered a curse and lowered his head to capture her lips with his.

As his mouth moved over hers in a gentle caress, Callie's pulse raced and her insides began to hum. The last thing she'd expected for him to do was kiss her. But instead of pushing him away as she should have, she reached out and placed her hands on his biceps to steady herself. The feel of his rock-hard muscles flexing beneath her palms sent a shiver of excitement up her spine and caused her knees to tremble.

If she had any sense, she'd put a stop to the kiss right now and demand that he leave. But his firm, warm lips were making her feel things that she'd only read about in women's magazines and romance novels, and she didn't want the delicious sensations to end.

When he wrapped his arms around her and pulled her against him to deepen the kiss, the feel of his superior strength surrounding her sent tiny little sparks skipping over every nerve in her body. Opening for him, she felt her heart skip several beats when he slipped his tongue inside to tease and explore her with a tenderness that made forming a coherent thought all but impossible.

Placing his hand at the small of her back, he urged her forward, but the feel of her round little tummy pressed to his stomach must have brought him back to reality. He suddenly went completely still, then, releasing her, he carefully set her away from him and took a couple of steps back.

"That shouldn't…have happened." He ran an agitated hand through his thick dark brown hair. "I think I should probably leave."

"Don't worry about it."

Embarrassed and more than a little confused by her uncharacteristic behavior, Callie began packing more cookies into the plastic containers. Why hadn't she stopped him instead of clinging to him as if she were desperate for a man's attention?

Hunter O'Banyon might be tall, dark and movie-star handsome, but she was no more interested in him than she was in any other man. But, dear heaven above, could he ever kiss.

Her cheeks feeling as if they were on fire from her sudden wayward thought, she shoved a container of cookies into his hands. "Take these back to the hangar for Mary Lou and the on-duty crew."

"Callie…I—"

If he didn't leave soon, she'd be up all night baking. "It's getting late and I'm sure you need to get back." She walked into the living room and opened the front door. "Thank you for stopping by. I appreciate your concerns and I will give them some thought."

"By the way, I know this is short notice, but I'm holding a staff meeting the day after tomorrow at 10:00 a.m.," he said, looking anything but happy. "Will you be able to be there?"

She shook her head. "I have a doctor's appointment. But I'll stop by after my checkup and someone can fill me in on what was covered in the meeting."

He stared at her for what seemed an eternity before he gave her a short nod. "Good night, Callie," he said, walking out onto the porch.

"Have a nice rest of the evening, Hunter," she said, closing the door behind him.

Walking straight to the kitchen, she stacked the containers of cookies on a shelf in her freezer, then pulled out the ingredients for a batch of brownies. Her phone conversation with her mother had been frustrating and caused her to make several batches of cookies. But Hunter's disturbing kiss was sending her into a baking frenzy, and for some odd reason everything she wanted to make was chocolate.

As she measured cocoa and flour, something she'd heard on a cooking show came to mind and caused her to knock over a cup of sugar. Eating chocolate released the same endorphins in the brain that were released while having sex.

"Not good, Callie. Not good at all."

Hurriedly opening a bag of milk-chocolate chips, she popped a handful into her mouth, and as the rich taste spread over her tongue, she decided that even if chocolate did make her gain too much weight, it was far less dangerous to her peace of mind than Hunter O'Banyon.

As he descended the steps and walked over to the white truck with Life Medevac painted on the side, Hunter shook his head. He didn't blame Callie one damned bit for giving him the bum's rush. Hell, he'd deserved more than that. He'd acted like an oversexed teenager on his first date. But what he was having the devil of a time trying to figure out was why.

Getting into the truck, he started the engine and, backing from the driveway, drove across town. But instead of turning onto the road leading to the Life Medevac hangar, he kept going until the lights of Devil's Fork faded in the distance behind him. He needed to think, and even though he could go into his room for solitude, he'd found that staring at the vastness of a starlit night always helped him put things in perspective.

When he parked the truck and stared out the windshield at the stars above the Apache Mountains in the distance, he couldn't help but wonder what the hell had gotten into him. He'd only stopped by Callie's place to try to talk some sense into her and get her to see the wisdom in grounding herself until after she had her baby. But when he'd placed his hands on her shoulders and looked into her pretty violet eyes, he could no more have stopped himself from tasting her sweetness than he could stop his next breath.

He took a deep breath. Although he wasn't overly proud of it, he hadn't exactly led the life of a monk since Ellen's death. But he'd always been careful to be with women who wanted nothing more from him than mutual satisfaction and had no expectations of their liaison leading to anything more. And Callie Marshall was most definitely *not* that type of woman. Instead of smoke-filled nightclubs, champagne cocktails and a meaningless one-night stand, she was a cozy little cottage, homemade cookies and a long-term commitment.

But come to think of it, he'd been so busy in the past several months that he'd completely abandoned any kind of a social life. And although he was far from being as randy as a seventeen-year-old boy, a man of thirty-two did have certain needs that couldn't be ignored.

He frowned. But he'd never in his entire life found a pregnant woman irresistible.

He stared at a shooting star streaking across the inky sky. He guessed it was only natural that he'd be attracted to Callie even though she was expecting a baby, considering his current state of celibacy. She was a very pretty woman with a killer smile, a delightful laugh and a pair of legs that could drive a saint to sin. Combine all those traits with his neglected libido and it was no wonder he'd felt compelled to kiss her.

Satisfied that he'd discovered the reason for his un-characteristic caveman behavior, he started the truck and headed back toward the Life Medevac base. Now that he had things in perspective, there was no reason that he and Callie couldn't put what happened this evening behind them and move forward as employer and employee. Hell, maybe they could even be friends.

But much later, as he lay in bed trying to will himself to sleep, Hunter couldn't seem to forget the sweet taste of Callie's soft lips or that the blood in his veins had heated considerably when she'd kissed him back. And whether he liked it or not, the very last thing on his mind was friendship.

Three

On the drive back from her appointment with the obstetrician, Callie thought about Hunter's visit and how foolish she'd been. The kiss they'd shared had been very nice, but it didn't mean anything. She knew he'd been frustrated with her refusal to ground herself and he'd been just as surprised by his actions as she had. There had really been no reason for her to get so flustered and read more into it than that.

But she'd spent the rest of the night baking everything from chocolate-fudge-nut brownies to chocolate cake. And by the time she'd gone to bed, the gray light of dawn had begun to chase away the shadows of night.

She shook her head. She hadn't baked that much since she'd discovered she was pregnant.

Thinking back on that day, she could still remember walking out of her gynecologist's office in a total state of shock. She'd always wanted children, but she'd envisioned herself happily married and anticipating the blessed event with the man she loved and who loved her in return. She wasn't supposed to have become pregnant by a man who put social status above a meaningful relationship.

When she'd first met Craig Culbertson, he'd swept her off her feet with his charm and thoughtfulness. But it hadn't taken long for her to discover that he wasn't the man she'd thought he was. He'd hidden his true nature behind a winning smile and charming ways, and by the time they'd parted company, *shallow, self-centered* and *selfish* were the nicest words she could think of to describe the conceited snake.

Then, when she'd discovered she was pregnant a month after their breakup, her disillusionment with Craig had turned to abject fear. One of the deciding factors in her ending their relationship had been the sickening disgust she'd felt when he'd confided in her that at the age of nineteen he'd gotten his girlfriend pregnant and that his twelve-year-old brother was actually his son. He'd told her that once his parents had learned of the pregnancy and discovered the girl wasn't the family's social equal, they'd used their money, as well as their position in Houston society, to gain custody of the baby, adopt him and raise the boy as their own.

A cold chill raced through Callie. She could only imagine the devastation and powerlessness the young mother must have felt at losing all contact with her child. And that was the very reason Callie had made the decision to leave her job as an emergency room nurse at one of the Houston hospitals and take the job as flight nurse with Life Medevac.

If Craig found out about her pregnancy, she wasn't sure he and his parents wouldn't try to do the same thing to her that they'd done to the mother of his first child. Callie hadn't been born into a life of wealth and privilege and therefore would no doubt be considered an undesirable candidate to raise a Culbertson heir. They'd take her to court and she'd come out the loser. She didn't have the kind of money it would take to fight a custody battle against their high-powered lawyers.

She'd come from a middle-class single-parent home where there hadn't been an endless supply of money, and social outings had consisted of making trips to the mall or attending a matinee at the movie theater. And even if her father hadn't been lost at sea during a storm while working on an oil platform in the Gulf of Mexico, her social status wouldn't have been a whole lot different.

As she steered her car onto the lane leading up to

the Life Medevac hangar, she placed her hand on her rounded tummy. She might not have been born with a silver spoon in her mouth, but she loved her little boy with all her heart, and no one was going to take him away from her.

Parking the car, she took a deep breath and forced herself to forget about Houston and the ruthless Culbertsons. She was about to face Hunter O'Banyon and tell him that she'd given a lot of thought to his request that she ground herself. She'd even gone so far as to discuss her physical limitations with her obstetrician, and together they'd concluded there was no reason for her to go on maternity leave for a few more months. Now all she had to do was explain that to Hunter.

"Hi, Mary Lou," Callie said as she entered the dispatch room. "Is Hunter in his office?"

The older woman nodded. "I suspect he's back there compiling a list of everyone's size and the number of new flight suits he's going to order." She laughed. "How do you look in red?"

"We're going to wear red flight suits?"

"That's what he says." Mary Lou looked thoughtful. "Come to think of it, though, our crews will be more easily identified among other emergency personnel at an accident scene."

"It does get confusing sometimes when some of the other services wear the same shade of dark blue that we do," Callie agreed.

"Did everything go okay at the doctor's office?" Mary Lou asked. Since learning of Callie's pregnancy, the woman had taken it upon herself to monitor Callie's progress and well-being.

Smiling, Callie nodded. "The obstetrician did a sonogram and said the baby's size is right on target for a four-and-a-half-month fetus." She laughed. "But I doubt that I can get away with blaming my five-pound weight gain on my son."

"No, that would be due to all those cookies you bake," Mary Lou said, grinning.

As Callie walked down the hall to Hunter's office, she decided that Mary Lou was right. If she didn't stop baking, there wouldn't be a flight suit big enough to accommodate her expanding form, whether she was pregnant or not.

Knocking on Hunter's office door, she waited a moment before entering the office. "Do you have the time to fill me in on what took place at the staff meeting or should I come back later?"

He shook his head and pointed to the brown leather chair in front of his desk. "Have a seat. I've been waiting for you."

"That sounds ominous."

"Not really." His intense green eyes held hers as she lowered herself into the oversize armchair and tried not to notice how good-looking he was or that the sound of his deep voice had caused her insides to start humming. "Before I can order the new flight suits for everyone, I need to know if you've given any more thought to my suggestion that you ground yourself until after your baby is born."

"Yes, I have." She met his questioning gaze head-on. "I even discussed your concerns with my obstetrician this morning."

"And?"

Hunter held out little hope that she'd changed her mind, but since it had been the uppermost thing on his mind for the past two days, he had to know.

"The doctor and I both agreed that as long as I avoid heavy lifting, eat a healthy diet and get plenty of rest, there's no reason that I can't continue as a flight nurse on the Evac II team."

"But—"

"But nothing." Her determined expression warned him that she wasn't going to budge on the issue. "I'm not only capable of doing my job, I need the money I'll make between now and when I give birth to pay for the doctor and hospital."

He had to concentrate hard to keep his mind off the fact that she had the prettiest violet eyes he'd ever seen. "And there's nothing I can say to change your mind?"

"No. But as I told you the other night, if my continuing to fly bothers you that much, pair me with your best pilot. That should eliminate some of your concerns about pilot error."

Hunter took a deep breath, then slowly released it as resignation set in. "I anticipated your decision and I've already made arrangements for you and Corey to be switched to Evac I."

"That's your team." If the dismay on her pretty face was any indication, he'd shocked her.

Not at all happy about the situation, he nodded. "George and Mike—the Evac III pilot—are good, but I'm better."

"Don't you think your assumption that you're a better pilot is a bit arrogant?" She didn't look any happier with his decision than he was.

He shook his head. "Not in the least. It's a matter of experience. I have more flight hours in a Bell helicopter than George and Mike combined. Until he retired from the Air Force a couple of years ago, George flew Sikorskys. And Mike flew Apaches for the Army. I've flown a Bell almost exclusively for the past twelve years." He stopped short at adding that if he'd been behind the controls of a Bell the day of the accident, instead of a reconditioned military chopper given to the hurricane relief organization for aid missions, his fiancée would probably still be alive.

"When does this reassignment take place?"

"Effective immediately." Glancing down at the list of everyone's flight suit sizes, he asked, "What size flight suit do you think you'll need until after you have the baby?"

As he watched her thoughtfully nibble on her lower lip, sweat popped out on his forehead. The memory of Callie's softness and sweet taste when he'd kissed her was doing a real number on his neglected libido.

Giving him the size she thought she'd need to accommodate her advancing pregnancy, she asked, "Was there anything else discussed during the staff meeting that I should know about?"

He sat back in his desk chair. "Mary Lou served your cookies, and everyone agreed that if you ever decide to give up nursing, you should open a bakery shop."

She gave him a half smile as she stood up. "I don't think that would be a good idea. I only bake when I'm…" She stopped suddenly and shook her head. "It doesn't matter. What's my new schedule?"

Hunter rose to his feet. "Instead of coming in this evening, you'll need to be here day after tomorrow."

"At the usual time? Or did you change that, too?"

"Six in the evening," he said, nodding. When she turned toward the door, he said, "By the way, the other night I noticed you have a loose board on one of the porch steps. You'd better have your landlord fix it. You don't want to run the risk of falling."

"If I had a landlord, I'd have him take care of the repair." She shrugged one slender shoulder. "But since I bought the place when I moved to Devil's Fork, I guess I'll have to buy a hammer and a few nails and see what I can do about it myself."

For reasons he didn't care to contemplate, he didn't like the idea of her trying to make the repair herself. "I'll be over this evening to fix the step."

"Don't worry about it." She edged toward the door. "Upkeep is part of a homeowner's job. I don't think hammering a couple of nails into a board will be all that difficult."

Hunter figured he knew what the problem was and, rounding the desk, walked over and put his hands on her slender shoulders. He realized he'd made a huge error in judgment the moment he touched her. An electric charge zinged straight up his arms, and he had to fight an overwhelming urge to draw her closer.

"Callie, about the other night—"

"Please, don't." She shook her head. "It was just a simple kiss and I'm sure it didn't mean anything more to you than it did to me."

Whether it was a matter of stung pride, a bruised ego or the fact that he hadn't been able to forget how soft and yielding she'd been in his arms, her statement hit like a physical blow and he was determined to prove her wrong. "Darlin', that kiss was anything but simple." Slowly lowering his head, he felt as though he just might drown in her violet eyes. "And I think you know it as well as I do."

The moment his lips touched hers, it felt as if a spark ignited somewhere deep inside of him and heat spread throughout his entire body. If he had any sense at all, he'd call Emerald Larson, tell her that he'd changed his mind about taking over the air-ambulance service and put as much distance as he could between himself and Callie Marshall.

But instead of setting her away from him and apologizing for acting like an oversexed teenager, Hunter slid his arms around her and pulled her to him. Callie's soft, petite body nestled against his much larger frame sent blood racing through his veins and caused his heart to pound hard against his rib cage.

When her perfect lips parted on a soft sigh, he took advantage of her acquiescence and deepened the kiss. Slipping his tongue inside, he tasted the sweetness that was uniquely Callie and reacquainted himself with her tender inner recesses.

To his satisfaction, she circled his waist with her arms and melted against him as he gently coaxed her into doing a little exploring of her own. But with each stroke of her tongue to his, the fire that had begun to burn in his belly spread lower and his body tightened with desire faster than he could have ever imagined.

Shocked by the intensity of his need, he eased away from the kiss. Staring at the confusion on her pretty face, he had a feeling he looked just as bewildered.

"I, um, think...it might be a good idea...if we didn't do that again," she said, sounding suspiciously breathless.

"I think you're right." Releasing her, he rubbed at

the tension gathering at the base of his neck. Why did he turn into a Neanderthal every time he was around her? "I'll…see you later this evening…when I come by to repair the step."

She hurried over to the door. "It's really not necessary. I can handle fixing the—"

"I said I'd take care of it." He shook his head. "I can still fly a helicopter with a swollen finger. But if you smash your thumb, you'll have trouble starting an IV or splinting a broken limb."

She stared at him for several more seconds before she nodded, then quickly walked out of his office.

As Hunter watched Callie leave, he closed his eyes and counted to ten, then twenty. Why the hell couldn't he have left well enough alone? What on God's green earth had he thought he was going to prove, besides the fact that he had all the finesse of a bulldozer? Hadn't he sorted through what happened the other night and come to a reasonable conclusion for his attraction to her?

He hadn't been with a woman in almost a year, and that was long enough to make any normal adult male ready to crawl the walls. But even as he thought about finding a willing little lady to help him scratch his itch, he rejected the idea. A one-night stand might help him with his basic needs, but a meaningless encounter couldn't fill the void of companionship in his life.

Shaking his head, he walked back to his desk and sank into his chair. He wasn't looking for any kind of romantic relationship and neither was Callie, but he saw no reason why they couldn't be friends. They were both new in town, alone, and she needed someone to help out with the upkeep on her house from time to time.

Now if he could just keep that in mind and stop grabbing her like a caveman and kissing her until they both needed CPR, everything would be just fine.

As he sat there trying to convince himself that he could do just that, the phone rang. Checking the caller ID, he groaned when he recognized one of Emerald Larson's private numbers.

Switching the speakerphone on, he greeted his grandmother. "Hello, Emerald."

"Good afternoon, Hunter. How is my oldest grandson?"

He almost laughed. He wasn't fool enough to think that the old gal had called him just to say hello and shoot the breeze. Emerald Larson had a purpose behind everything she did. And that included placing a phone call to one of her grandsons.

"I'm doing okay. How are you?"

"Planning a little dinner party for my grandsons and their wives for the end of next month." She paused. "You will attend, won't you?"

"Sure," Hunter said, suddenly feeling more alone than he had in his entire life.

He'd only learned about his brothers a few months

ago, and although they'd formed a bond of friendship that he knew would stand the test of time, Caleb and Nick had both recently married. And that made Hunter the odd man out. Unfortunately he'd always be the odd man out. Marriage and family weren't in the cards for him. Not now. Not in the future.

Loving someone only opened a person up to more pain and heartache than it was worth. His mother had loved Owen Larson and ended up suffering a lifetime of loneliness for her efforts. Owen had run out on her, to leave her facing motherhood alone, and never looked back when he returned to Harvard after sweeping her off her feet during his spring-break in Miami. Then, Hunter had damned near lost his mind from the guilt of surviving the helicopter crash that had taken the lives of Ellen and their unborn child.

No, the emotional investment and risks that went along with loving someone weren't worth the high price a man had to pay.

"Hunter, are you still there?"

"Sorry." He took a deep breath. "What was that you were saying?"

"I said I'm on my way back to Wichita from Houston and I thought I would stop by to see you and my old friend Mary Lou."

He should have known that she wouldn't be able to resist checking up on him from time to time. She'd done the same with his brothers and the companies she'd given them. Why should he be any different?

Even though she'd given him Life Medevac to run as he saw fit, it still came under the umbrella of Emerald Inc., and she hadn't become one of the richest, most successful businesswomen in the world by sitting back and letting others oversee her holdings.

"When will you be here?" he asked, barely resisting the urge to cuss a blue streak.

"My pilot said we should be landing at the Devil's Fork airfield in five minutes."

Rubbing the tension at the base of his neck, Hunter sighed heavily. "I'll be there in a few minutes to pick you up."

"There's no need." He could envision her waving her bejeweled hand dismissively. "I had a limousine service send a car down from Odessa to drive me to the Life Medevac hangar."

"Then I guess I'll see you shortly," he said, resigned to his fate of spending the afternoon with his indomitable grandmother.

Fifteen minutes later, when he met the limousine in the Life Medevac parking lot, Hunter wasn't surprised to see Luther Freemont, Emerald's trusted personal assistant, standing ramrod-straight beside the open back door of a sleek black limousine. "Hey there, Luther. How's it going?"

"Very well, sir," the man answered, as formal as

ever. Once he helped Emerald from the backseat of the limo, he gave Hunter a short nod. "It was nice seeing you again, sir."

When his grandmother slipped her hand in the crook of Hunter's arm and started walking toward the office entrance, he noticed that her assistant got back into the limo. "Do you think old Luther will be all right out here on his own? After all, this place is to hell and gone from a corporate office."

"Poor Luther, he's a proper gentleman and very set in his ways." Emerald laughed. "He doesn't quite know what to make of you and your brothers."

"The feeling's mutual."

"And he's not at all sure what to think of southwest Texas."

Hunter opened the door and waited for her to precede him into the building. "Is Luther always such a tight…uptight?"

As she laughed, her silver-gray eyes twinkled merrily. "Yes, he's always very formal."

"I'll bet he was just a barrel of laughs when he was a kid," Hunter said as he escorted Emerald into the dispatch room.

He introduced her to the on-duty Evac III team as they passed through on the way to his private office, but purposely avoided calling her his grandmother. He still wasn't entirely comfortable thinking of her as a family member, nor did he need the added pressure that went along with others knowing he was her grandson.

"Where's Mary Lou?" she asked, seating herself in the chair in front of his desk.

"When she found out you were dropping by, she decided to run into town to pick up something for refreshments. She'll be back soon."

"Good. I haven't seen her in quite some time and I'm looking forward to catching up."

As they stared at each other across the desk, Hunter couldn't help but think how out of place Emerald Larson looked. She was professional elegance from the top of her perfectly styled silver hair to the soles of her Italian pumps. His office furnishings were light-years away from the opulence she surrounded herself with at Emerald Inc. headquarters.

"A few months ago, when you learned I'm your grandmother and I told you about your father, you weren't as vocal about your feelings as your brothers, Caleb and Nick."

She gave him a look that he had no doubt intimidated the hell out of anyone facing her in a corporate boardroom. But he wasn't one of her loyal lackeys and she was on his turf now.

"I'm here to clear the air once and for all," she said bluntly.

"Do we have to?" he asked before he could stop

himself. He knew for certain she wouldn't want to hear what he thought of her interference in his life.

"Yes." There was a steely determination in her voice, and whether he liked it or not, he knew come hell or high water she was going to have her say. "I'm sure you'd like to know why I insisted that your mother keep her silence about your father's identity until I was ready to tell you myself."

He glared at the woman who until three months ago he'd known only by reading about her in newspapers and national magazines. He hated dancing to her tune. But as his mother had pointed out before he'd left Miami, if he hadn't taken Emerald up on her offer of giving him one of her companies to run, the sacrifices she'd made to ensure his birthright would have been in vain. Keeping his father's identity a secret from her close-knit Irish family had caused a breach that had never been reconciled.

Hunter clenched his back teeth together so tightly his jaw ached. "I'm still having a problem with that. What gave you the right to coerce my mother into signing a paper stating that she wouldn't tell anyone— not even me—who my father was?"

"I know you're bitter about the way I handled everything," Emerald said patiently. "I'd probably feel the same way. But believe me, it was the best for all concerned parties."

Anger, swift and hot, burned at his gut. "For who? You or your son?"

"I never once considered the effect it would have on me or Owen." She shrugged. "My only concern was you and your mother."

"What you did to my mother, as well as to Caleb's and Nick's mothers, amounts to blackmail." He hadn't meant to sound so harsh, but the truth wasn't always pretty.

To his surprise, Emerald didn't seem the least bit offended by his accusation. "You see it as blackmail. I saw it as protecting my grandsons and their mothers from the hazards of dealing with the paparazzi and a corruptive lifestyle." She sighed. "I was determined to see that you and your brothers didn't turn out to be anything like your father. Owen might be alive today if I had given him more of my time and attention instead of everything he thought he wanted."

Hunter took a deep breath in an attempt to bring his temper under control. "Did he even know that he'd gotten three women pregnant?"

For the first time since meeting the mighty Emerald Larson and learning that she was his grandmother, Hunter watched her lower her head as if she might be ashamed of her philandering offspring. He could almost feel sorry for her. Almost.

"Yes, Owen knew he had three sons. But, as usual, he relied on me to bail him out of taking responsibility for his actions." When she raised her eyes to look at him there was unapologetic defiance in their gray depths. "I'll admit that I've made a lot of mistakes and have more than my share of regrets, but whether or not you approve of my methods to insure you boys were nothing like him, you can't deny that it worked. And I didn't exactly coerce your mother into signing the agreement to remain silent about your father. I just made it clear that should word get out that I'm your grandmother, I would have to deny it in order to protect you from the media frenzy it would create."

Hunter could see her reasoning, but that didn't change the fact that she'd waited thirty-two years before she'd clued him in on who had fathered him or that all that time she'd had private investigators reporting his and his brothers' every move. "Why did you wait so long to tell us?"

"I wanted all three of you to gain some life experiences of your own instead of having to live down your father's reputation of being an international playboy," she said pragmatically. "That would have been a huge burden for all of you. Not to mention how it would have affected you to learn that you had a multimillion-dollar trust fund and would eventually inherit a sizable part of my business holdings."

As Hunter mulled over what she'd said, he couldn't help but agree with her. Handling the knowledge that he'd become an overnight millionaire and owner of his own business was hard enough to grasp at the age of thirty-two. He couldn't imagine the effect it would have had on him at a much earlier age.

But before he could comment, Emerald added, "And before you ask, it was extremely hard for me to read about your accomplishments in a private investigator's report while you were growing up and not be there to see them for myself." She leaned forward as if to emphasize her point. "What I did and the way I went about it I did out of love. Believe me, nothing would have pleased me more than to have had a traditional grandmother's relationship with you and your brothers. But I had to give that up in order to protect you."

Thinking it over, Hunter realized that as difficult as it had been for him growing up not knowing who his father was, it had to have been much harder for Emerald. She'd known all about him and his brothers but hadn't been able to let any of them know how she felt.

"I guess all we can do now is move forward," he said, thinking aloud.

"I believe that would be wise," Emerald agreed. "Taking over the Life Medevac Helicopter Service is a good start for you, and I expect you to do quite well." She surprised him when she rose from the chair and rounded the desk to kiss his cheek. "It's time to get back to what you do best—flying helicopters and helping those in need—and leave the past behind,

Hunter. It's history and can't be changed. But the future is an unwritten page and sometimes found where you least expect it."

Four

"If you don't stop letting Hunter O'Banyon kiss you, you're going to be as big as a barn," Callie muttered, poking another snickerdoodle into her mouth as she measured the ingredients for a double batch of chocolate-chocolate-chip cookies.

The minute she'd arrived back home from her meeting with Hunter, she'd walked straight into the kitchen, put on her apron and started baking. Five dozen snickerdoodles, a double batch of sugar cookies and a pan of brownies later, she still hadn't been able to forget how his lips had felt on hers. Warm, firm and deliciously male, his mouth could very easily be classified as a lethal weapon. At least for her.

Spooning chocolate dough onto cookie sheets, she wondered what there was about Hunter that caused her to abandon every ounce of common sense she possessed. All he had to do was touch her and she clung to him like a piece of plastic shrink-wrap on a hot plate.

She slid the pan of cookie dough into the oven and set the timer. Then, sitting down at the table while she waited on the cookies to bake, Callie stared off into space.

It wasn't uncommon for a woman in her second trimester to find herself feeling more sensual than ever before, but she didn't think her pregnancy hormones could account for the compelling attraction she experienced with Hunter. With just a look he could make her heart flutter. And when he touched her, she practically melted into a puddle at his feet. She hadn't had that kind of reaction to Craig, and he was her baby's father.

Lost in thought, it took her a moment to realize someone was knocking on her door. Hurrying to remove the pan of cookies from the oven, when she walked into the living room and opened the door, she found Hunter squatted down beside the steps. He had replaced the loose board with a new one and was pounding nails into the wood with no more than a couple of whacks with a hammer. She swallowed hard when she noticed how his bicep and the muscles in his forearm flexed with each blow.

"That should last a while," he said, straightening to his full height. "And it'll be a lot safer for you."

When she finally found her voice, she nodded. "Thank you."

He wiped the sweat from his forehead on the sleeve of his T-shirt. "Is there anything else that needs fixing or that you'd like me to take a look at while I'm here?"

"I can't think of anything." She motioned toward the door. "Would you like to come in to cool off and have a glass of iced tea?"

Smiling, he nodded. "That sounds like a winner." He put the hammer and a small sack of nails in the back of his truck, then climbed the steps to Callie's cottage. "It's not as humid here in southwest Texas as it is in Florida, but it's still hotter than hell."

Callie laughed as they walked inside the house. "It's late August. What do you expect?"

"Good point," he said, grinning.

When they walked into the kitchen, she poured them each a glass of iced tea. "Having lived close to the Gulf all my life, I'm not used to all this dry heat."

"Thank God for air-conditioning."

"Amen to that." She smiled as she placed her hand on her rounded stomach. "I've been hotter this summer than I've ever been in my life."

"It's no wonder you're hot, with the oven on all the time." Chuckling, he looked at the plates of cookies and brownies sitting on the counter. "I see you've been at it again."

She smiled wanly. There was no way she was going to tell him that just the thought of him kissing her could send her into a baking frenzy.

He reached for a brownie. "What are you going to do with all this stuff?"

Thinking quickly, she shrugged. "Schools are always having bake sales. I thought I'd donate some of the things I've baked for their fund-raisers. And after the baby is born, I doubt that I'll have a lot of time, so I've frozen a lot of what I've made."

"Good idea." He grinned. "I'm sure Corey will appreciate that."

"I'm sure he will. He eats constantly but never seems to fill up." She frowned. "Do all boys eat like they have a bottomless pit for a stomach?"

"Pretty much." Hunter reached for one of the chocolate-chocolate-chip cookies on the baking sheet she'd removed from the oven earlier. "My mom said that once I hit puberty, I ate everything in sight."

"I guess that's something I have to look forward to." Callie smiled at the fluttering in her stomach. It was as if the baby knew she was talking about him.

"You're having a boy?"

She nodded. "That's what the sonogram indicates."

"When are you due?"

"Around the first of the year." She turned to spoon cookie dough onto a baking sheet. "Of course, that doesn't mean he won't decide to come a couple of weeks early or late."

"That would be anywhere from a week or so before Christmas to mid-January."

She wondered why Hunter was taking such an interest in when she'd give birth, until it occurred to her that he would need to find someone to cover her shifts at Life Medevac. "I'm planning on taking maternity leave at Thanksgiving and being back to work no later than mid-February. Mary Lou suggested that I bring the baby to work with me and she could watch him when I go out on a call. Is that all right with you?"

He nodded. "But are you sure it's a good idea to wait that long to take your leave?" He frowned. "I don't mean to offend you, but won't it be difficult climbing in and out of the helicopter when you're that…far along?"

"No offense taken. I know I'll be quite large." She slipped the pan of cookies into the oven, then turned to face him. "If I see that it's a problem, I'll…take my leave earlier than…I'd planned."

He took a step toward her. "Are you all right?"

Laughing, she nodded. "It's just the baby moving. He seems to be particularly active today."

"Does it hurt?" He looked and sounded genuinely concerned.

"No. If anything, it tickles." She lovingly placed her hand on her stomach. "At this stage of pregnancy it's like having a butterfly flapping its wings inside of me. Later on, I'm told it will feel like I have a prizefighter in there."

"I'll bet that does feel weird." When the timer on the oven went off, he reached for a hot pad. "Why don't you sit down and put your feet up?"

"I'm fine."

Hunter pointed to one of the kitchen chairs. "Sit."

He could tell she wasn't happy about it, but while she sat down and propped her feet up in one of the other chairs, he removed the cookies from the oven. "Damn! That's hot!" he cursed when the back of his hand touched the top of the oven.

She was at his side in a flash. "Let me see."

Reluctantly letting her examine his hand, he tried to ignore how nice her soft palms felt holding his calloused one. "It's nothing."

"It's already starting to form a blister," she said, reaching for a bottle of some kind of clear lotion.

"What's that?"

"Aloe vera. It will stop it from hurting and help it heal faster." She flipped the top of the bottle open, then glanced up at him and grinned. "And don't worry, it won't make you smell like a flower."

As he watched her gently spread the clear gel on the small burn, a warmth began to fill his chest. It had been a long time since he'd had a woman fussing over him. And whether it was wise or not, he liked the feeling more than he cared to admit.

"That should take care of it," she said, closing the bottle.

Amazed at how much better it felt, he flexed his hand. "That stuff really works. Thanks."

"Not...a problem."

She sounded slightly winded, and he figured their close proximity had the same effect on her that it had on him. He was having the devil of a time trying to keep from taking her in his arms and kissing her senseless.

"I think I'd better be going."

"How much do I owe you for fixing the step?" she asked, reaching for her purse on the table.

"I ate enough cookies and brownies to more than pay for the job."

He edged toward the door. If he didn't get out of there soon, he was going to take her in his arms—and that could spell disaster to his good intentions. And he'd have succeeded, too, if she hadn't touched him.

"Hunter, stop being so darned stubborn."

Her small hand resting on his forearm sent a wave of heat streaking throughout his entire body. Without a single thought to the consequences or that he'd promised himself he'd be able to keep his hands to himself, he pulled her into his arms.

"Darlin', friends help each other all the time." He

kissed her forehead. "And they don't ask for anything in return."

She stared at him for several long seconds before she shook her head. "I'm not sure that you and I could ever be just friends. And right now I'm not looking for anything more."

"That makes two of us, Callie." He brushed her perfect lips with his. "But I think as long as we keep that in mind, we'll be just fine." He kissed her soundly, then forced himself to set her away from him and walk to the door. Turning back, he smiled. "I'll see you at work tomorrow evening, *friend.*"

"Where's Corey?" Callie asked when she arrived at work the next evening. "I didn't see his truck in the parking lot."

"He called to say he'd be a few minutes late," Mary Lou answered as she opened the container of brownies Callie had placed on the table by the coffeepot. Removing a double-fudge-and-nut chocolate square, she took a bite and shrugged. "I told him that if we get a call before he reports for his shift, I'd give him a talkin' to he won't soon forget."

Callie frowned. "It's not like Corey to be late. Did he say what's up?"

"He said he and his girlfriend were on their way back from talking to her parents up in Odessa. He should be here in about a half hour or so." Mary Lou lowered her voice and leaned forward. "Can you keep a secret?"

"Of course."

The older woman grinned. "Corey is going to be a daddy in about seven months."

"You're kidding." Callie laughed. "He's not much more than a boy himself."

Mary Lou grinned. "I've always said he's twenty-two going on ten."

"What's up?" Hunter asked, walking into the dispatch room.

Callie's heart came to a skittering halt, then took off double time. If she'd thought he looked good in jeans and a T-shirt, it was nothing compared to the way he looked in his flight suit. The one-piece coverall emphasized the impossible width of his muscular shoulders and narrowness of his trim waist.

"Just some girl talk," Mary Lou said, winking at Callie.

"Which one of us guys are you dissecting?" Hunter asked, grinning.

His comment had been for both she and Mary Lou, but when his gaze caught Callie's, she felt warm all the way to her toes. If he wanted to, she had a feeling Hunter O'Banyon could charm a little old lady right out of her garters with that smile of his.

And he thought they could be *just* friends? She

almost laughed. The way he was looking at her, there was a better chance of elephants roosting in trees.

"Don't worry, big guy." Mary Lou cackled. "We weren't taking you to task for anything. This time."

He arched one dark eyebrow. "This time?"

"We were discussing when Corey would show up," Callie added.

Hunter's skeptical expression turned to one of understanding. "Corey had some important personal business to take care of up in Odessa. He'll be here as soon as he can."

"You know what's going on, don't you?" Callie guessed.

"He came by yesterday evening to ask me and Mike what we thought he should do about the situation," Hunter said, nodding.

"That little skunk told me I was the only one he'd talked to about it," Mary Lou said, obviously put out that the confidence wasn't as big a secret as she'd thought. "Just wait until I—" Mary Lou stopped abruptly when the emergency phone rang.

Callie listened as Mary Lou asked several questions in Spanish. Great. Corey wasn't back yet and on the Evac II team he'd been the only one fluent in Spanish.

"Come on, Callie. We don't have time to wait for Corey," Hunter said, heading for the door. "As it is, we're going to have to race the stork to the hospital."

"Is it Juanita Rodriguez again?" Callie asked,

thankful that Hunter had obviously understood Mary Lou's end of the conversation and would be able to interpret for her.

He nodded as they climbed into the helicopter and put on the headsets that would enable them to communicate over the engine noise. "She's definitely in labor this time. From Mary Lou's questions, I could tell that Juanita's water broke and she's home alone."

"Where's her husband Miguel?"

"He's in El Paso at a National Guard meeting this weekend. We can radio his armory and have him meet us at the hospital."

While Hunter started the engine, Callie strapped herself into one of the jump seats in the back and listened to Mary Lou's voice give the coordinates for the Rodriguez ranch to Hunter. They had about a fifteen-minute flight to reach their destination, then another thirty minutes on to El Paso. Mary Lou was going to stay on the phone with Juanita until they got there, and hopefully Baby Rodriguez would wait to make his or her grand entrance into the world until after they made it to the hospital.

When they lifted off, Callie began to mentally run through emergency birthing procedure on the outside chance that she would have to deliver Juanita's baby, and it took a moment for her to realize Hunter had spoken to her. "I'm sorry. What did you say?"

"I asked if you've delivered a baby before." His

deep baritone coming through the headset was oddly intimate and sent a shiver straight up her spine.

She gave herself a mental shake. Hearing Hunter's voice through the headset was no different than when she'd communicated with George or Corey on a flight.

"I've delivered a few babies—one of them in the back of a taxicab when the E.R. doctors were busy treating victims from a bus accident."

"But you don't speak or understand Spanish?"

She sighed. "No."

They fell silent, and in what seemed record time, Hunter was setting the helicopter down in a field next to the Rodriguez ranch house.

Removing her headset and unfastening her seat belt, Callie grabbed one of the medical cases containing sterile dressings, latex gloves and other medical supplies and hurriedly slid the side door back. She bent slightly to avoid the rotor blades, then, once she was clear of the helicopter, she jogged the short distance to the house. Fortunately the front door was unlocked, and she walked inside without so much as a second thought.

"*¡Por favor ayúdeme!*"

Callie followed the frantic cries and found Juanita in one of the bedrooms. Drenched in sweat, the young woman was practically hysterical and instead of working with the contractions she seemed to be fighting them.

"*¡El bebé está listo!*" Juanita repeated, clutching at Callie's hands.

"What's she saying about the baby?" Callie asked Hunter when he appeared in the narrow doorway.

"She said the baby is ready."

"Tell her that I need to check to see how close she is to having the baby," Callie said, slipping on a pair of sterile latex gloves.

While Hunter assured Juanita that everything was going to be all right, Callie checked to see how many centimeters the woman had dilated. "The stork is going to win this one," she said, reaching into the medical case for clamps, a sterile drape and antiseptic. "The baby's head is crowning."

As she arranged the medical supplies she would need for the birth of Juanita's baby, Callie listened to Hunter reassure the woman. She had no idea what he was telling her, but it seemed to calm Juanita as well as send warmth throughout Callie's body. She'd always thought Spanish was a beautiful language and she didn't think she'd ever heard a more sexy sound than Hunter's deep voice flawlessly pronouncing the words.

"Do you have any kind of experience being a breathing coach?" Callie asked as she prepped Juanita for the delivery.

He shook his head. "No. We covered it briefly in EMT training, but that's it."

"You'll do fine." Using the two-way radio clipped to the epaulet on the shoulder of her jumpsuit, she advised the hospital in El Paso of the situation, then turned her full attention on the task at hand. "Tell Juanita to breathe, then show her how. She's tensing up instead of relaxing her pelvic floor and allowing the baby to pass through the birth canal."

"*Respira,* Juanita. *Respira.*"

When Hunter showed the young woman what he meant, she trustingly stared into his eyes and began to concentrate on doing as he requested. Once she stopped fighting the pain, she rapidly progressed to the pushing phase of the delivery. Moving into position to lift her shoulders when it came time to push, he continued to reassure her that everything was going to be all right.

"*Todo será bien,* Juanita."

"Tell her to stop the shallow breathing and start pushing," Callie said, showing the woman how to position her hands on her knees for leverage.

Encouraging Juanita to push with all her might, he supported her shoulders, and after only a couple of tries, the baby's dark head emerged from the young woman's lower body. Hunter watched Callie quickly and efficiently suction the infant's nose and mouth before it was time for Juanita to push the rest of her baby out into the world.

With one more mighty push from Juanita, the baby slid out into Callie's waiting hands. Without being prompted, the baby girl opened her mouth and wailed at the top of her tiny lungs.

"*Mí bebé,*" Juanita murmured tearfully.

"You have a beautiful daughter, Juanita," Callie said, placing the baby on her mother's stomach.

Awed by the miracle he'd just witnessed, the moment was so bittersweet Hunter couldn't have pushed words past the lump clogging his throat if his life depended on it. Although he was happy for the Rodriguez family and their new addition, he'd never know what it was like to watch his own son or daughter come into the world. After losing Ellen and their unborn child, he never intended to put himself in the position of loving someone and taking the risk of losing them. He'd been down that road before and had barely survived. There was no way in hell he could go through that again.

"Hunter, could you please hold the baby while I get Juanita ready for transport?" Callie asked, breaking into his disturbing thoughts.

The last thing he wanted to do was hold a baby. He knew for certain it would only compound his sense of loss and regret that he'd never hold his own child. But before he could protest, Callie placed the baby in his arms. As he stared down at the red-faced little girl wrapped in a soft white blanket, instead of the sorrow he expected, Hunter couldn't help but marvel at how small she was, how perfect.

Gently touching her little hand, he was thoroughly amazed when the baby curled her perfectly formed tiny fingers around one of his. "She's holding on to me."

"Babies do that," Callie said, smiling.

He watched Callie and Juanita exchange an indulgent glance. Apparently there was no language barrier when it came to women's opinions of men. It must be universally accepted that men didn't have a clue about these things. But that was okay with him. Men didn't understand women, so he supposed that made the genders pretty equal.

While Callie radioed the hospital to report a successful, complication-free birth, Hunter contemplated how they were going to get Juanita into the helicopter without Corey. He wasn't about to let Callie lift anything heavier than her nurse's bag or the baby, and the door and hallway were too narrow to get the stretcher into the bedroom. That left only one alternative.

"Are we ready for transport?" When Callie nodded, he handed her the baby. "You take your nurse's bag and the baby while I carry Juanita to the chopper."

"That would probably be best," Callie said, lifting the nylon bag's webbed strap to her shoulder. "You'd probably have to carry her to the front door before you could put her on the stretcher anyway."

Telling Juanita what was taking place, Hunter scooped her slight body into his arms and carried her out to the helicopter. Once he placed her on the stretcher and Callie handed her the baby, Juanita and her new daughter both drifted off into a peaceful sleep.

The flight to El Paso was uneventful, and once they

had Juanita and her new daughter safely checked in to the hospital, Callie and Hunter boarded the helicopter and headed back to the Life Medevac base.

"You did a wonderful job of calming Juanita down," Callie said as she stared through the windshield at the vast blue sky ahead of them. Riding in the front seat next to Hunter on the trip back to Devil's Fork, she enjoyed the view of the rugged Texas mountains that she missed when riding in the back with a patient.

"It didn't show that I had no idea what I was doing?" he asked, grinning sheepishly.

Smiling, she shook her head. "Not at all. Juanita is young and had no idea what to expect when her contractions started. Factor in that she was home alone and miles away from help and it was no wonder she was frightened half out of her mind. You were able to put her at ease and that made it a lot easier for her."

He shrugged. "I just did what I thought would help." They were both silent for some time before he asked, "Who's going to be with you when you have your baby?"

It was the last thing she'd expected him to ask. "Are you volunteering for the job?"

"Hell no."

She laughed at his horrified expression. "But you're a great labor coach."

He grunted. "Only because Corey wasn't there to take over for me. I'm the pilot, remember?"

"You're also a certified EMT."

"Only because my grandmother strongly suggested that it would be a good idea since I was taking over an air-ambulance service." He shrugged. "Besides, whether or not you and the father of your baby are together, I'm sure he'll want to be there when his son is born. He can be your breathing coach."

A cold chill ran the length of her spine at the thought of Craig Culbertson being anywhere near her or her child. "I can assure you, he won't be anywhere around when I give birth."

"Maybe he'll change his mind."

"It's not an issue."

Hunter was quiet for a moment, then turned his head to give her a questioning look. "He doesn't even know he's fathered a child, does he?" His mouth flattening into a disapproving line, he shook his head. "Forget that I asked. It's none of my business."

She hadn't discussed with anyone—not even her mother—why she'd made the decision not to tell Craig about the baby. But she needed to make Hunter understand, without divulging too many details, why she felt she had no choice but to keep her silence.

"Believe me, it's for the best." Placing her hand protectively over her son, she shook her head. "Even if I told him about the baby, he wouldn't care."

"Don't you think you owe him the chance to prove you wrong?"

"No. He's too selfish and self-centered to care about anyone or anything but himself."

Hunter stared straight ahead and she could tell he was thinking over what she'd said. "There must have been some substance to the man or you wouldn't have become involved with him," he finally said.

Callie sighed heavily. "In the past several months I've spent countless hours wondering why I allowed myself to be fooled by his insincerity."

She could feel Hunter's intense gaze as surely as if he'd reached out and touched her. "And?"

"I came to the conclusion that he was the consummate charmer who was more interested in the chase than in a meaningful relationship."

"I know the type," Hunter said disgustedly. "Let me guess—he asked you out several times and you turned him down. That's when he pulled out all the stops and did everything in his power to convince you that he was wild about you."

"That's exactly what happened. I became a challenge that he was determined to conquer." She took a deep breath. "And like a fool, I allowed him to wear down my resistance and charm me into believing that we could have a future together."

When Hunter took her hand in his to give it a gentle squeeze, a warmth like nothing she'd ever known filled her all the way to her soul. "Don't be so hard on yourself, darlin'. It's not the first time a woman has been taken in by a player. And it's sad to say, but it won't be the last."

She knew he was right, but that didn't make her feel any less foolish for allowing it to happen, especially since she was now facing motherhood alone. "Then you understand my reasoning for keeping my pregnancy a secret?"

"Not entirely." He released her hand, then, remaining silent for several long seconds, he finally added, "Don't you think you should at least give him the opportunity to redeem himself? I know if I was in his shoes, I'd definitely be angry if I discovered a woman had denied me the right to know my own son."

Callie knew for certain she couldn't take the chance of telling Craig. But she wasn't ready to outline her reasons to Hunter. "He'd only view the baby as an inconvenience, and my child deserves better than that."

"Do you ever intend to tell your son who his father is?"

"He'll be better off not knowing."

"Every kid has a right to know who they are and where they came from," he said forcefully. His tone left no doubt that he felt very passionately about the subject. "He'll grow up wondering if every man he passes on the street is the one responsible for his existence."

"Why do you feel so strongly about this?"

She watched him take a deep breath, then slowly release it. Just when she thought he was going to tell her it was none of her concern, he spoke. "I grew up not knowing anything about my father, and it wasn't until just recently that I even learned who he was— after he'd been dead for six months."

"Oh, Hunter, I'm so sorry." She began to understand why he felt it was so important that she inform Craig about the baby. "Your mother didn't tell him about you?"

"He knew." There was an edge to his voice. "He just chose to ignore the fact that he'd fathered three sons with three different women." Hunter gave her a meaningful glance. "But the point is, they gave him the opportunity to know about us. He was the one who made the decision to stay out of our lives."

"But she didn't tell *you*," Callie guessed.

He shook his head. "She had her reasons and she knew that one day I would learn who he was. But that didn't make it any easier on me when I was growing up or stop me from resenting the fact that I wasn't given the choice to know anything about the man."

She could understand why Hunter felt the way he did, but her circumstances were different. If she told Craig about the baby, there was a good chance that he and his parents would try to separate her and her son the way they'd done that poor girl and her baby twelve years ago. And that was a chance Callie wasn't willing to take.

"I will tell my son about his father when I feel he's ready," she said carefully. "But until that time we'll be just fine on our own."

Five

For the next few days Hunter couldn't stop thinking about the conversation he'd had with Callie on the way back from El Paso. There'd been something in her voice that had alerted him to the fact there was more to her refusal to tell her baby's father about the pregnancy than she was letting on. He couldn't quite put his finger on what that something was, but it was serious enough that she felt silence was her only option.

Hunter's heart stalled. Could the man have been abusive?

Fury stronger than he could have ever imagined coursed through his veins. He wasn't a violent man by nature, but just the thought that the jerk might have mistreated Callie in any way was enough to make Hunter ready to tear him limb from limb.

Suddenly needing to move before he put his fist through the wall, Hunter grabbed his sunglasses and, taking his ball cap from a hook beside his office door, jammed it onto his head. He felt as if he had enough adrenaline coursing through him to bench-press a 747 fully loaded with passengers and cargo. What he needed was some good, hard physical labor to help him work off his anger. And he knew exactly what he was going to do.

As he drove to the lumber yard, he mentally reviewed all the things in need of repair or replacement at Callie's place. Besides the steps he'd fixed a few days ago, he'd noticed the place could use a coat of paint and a new deck at the back door to replace a badly deteriorating concrete stoop.

Purchasing everything he needed to make the improvements, Hunter scheduled a delivery for the lumber to build a new deck, then loaded his truck with a new extension ladder, several buckets of paint, brushes and scrapers. Satisfied that he had everything he needed, he headed toward Callie's house at the edge of town.

He'd thought about talking to her before he started buying supplies and making plans, but if her protest over the simple repair he'd made to the step was any indication, she would have refused his offer. And whether she liked it or not, he wasn't taking no for an answer. In the case of the back stoop, it was a matter of safety.

When he parked the truck and positioned the ladder against the side of the house, he wasn't surprised when she came out to glare at him. "Why on earth are you making so much noise and what are you doing to my house?"

With her shoulder-length blond hair in delightful disarray, her eyes soft with sleep and her feet bare, she looked as if she'd just crawled out of bed. She also looked sexy as hell.

"Good morning to you, too." He grinned as he grabbed one of the scrapers. "Did you stay up late last night making cookies?"

"As a matter of fact, I did."

"What kind?"

She shook her head. "Don't change the subject. What are you doing here at the god-awful hour of seven-thirty in the morning? And why is that ladder propped against the side of my house?"

"One thing at a time, darlin'," he said, climbing the ladder. "Contrary to popular belief, seven-thirty isn't all that early. Did you know the lumber yard and hardware store here in Devil's Fork open every morning at six?"

Glaring at him, she propped her fists on her shapely hips. "Since I've never had occasion to go into either establishment, no, I didn't know that."

He scraped off a long strip of peeling paint close to

the peak of the roof. "The other day I noticed that the paint on this place had started to crack and peel."

"So you just decided to take it upon yourself to paint my house?" Clearly fit to be tied, she looked mighty damned cute standing there in an oversize pink T-shirt and a pair of mint-green camp shorts, tapping her bare foot against the hard-packed dirt.

"You can't do it," he said as he continued to remove strips of weathered paint from the board siding. "And it needs to be done before winter sets in."

"It could wait until after I have the baby."

He shook his head. "You'll be too busy once the baby gets here. Besides, I might as well do something constructive on my days off."

"But I can't afford this right now."

"You don't have to pay for it."

"Yes, I do."

"I've already taken care of it."

She made a noise that sounded suspiciously like a growl. "Tell me how much you've spent and I'll pay you back."

He grinned. "Nope."

"Are you always this—" she stopped as if searching for the right word "—this meddlesome?"

He stopped scraping to stare down at her. "Are you always this stubborn when someone is trying to help you?"

Rubbing her temples with her fingertips, she shook

her head. "I do appreciate you trying to help. But I can't afford all the improvements right now and I can't let you pay for them."

"Consider it a housewarming gift," he said, sending more flakes of paint falling to the ground.

"That's absurd." She frowned. "You're newer in town than I am."

He chuckled. "Minor technicality."

"I can't let you do this."

"You can't stop me." He climbed down the ladder, then, placing the scraper on the tailgate of the truck, walked over to stand in front of her. "Look, there are things around here that need attention and you're not able to do them in your condition."

She rolled her eyes. "I've told you before, I'm pregnant, not disabled."

"Whatever. You can't do them and I need something to keep me busy on my days off."

He could tell he was wearing down her resistance when she sighed heavily. "Yes, but it isn't fair for you to pay for the materials to make improvements to my house."

Unable to resist taking her into his arms, he smiled as he pulled her to him, then pushed the brim of his ball cap up out of the way. "If it bothers you that much, why don't we strike a deal?"

She looked suspicious. "What kind of agreement are you talking about?"

"I'll do some work around your house and you can make me a few home-cooked meals." He used his index finger to raise her chin until their gazes met. "Does that sound fair?"

"Not really. I still think that I'm getting the better end of this deal."

Her soft body pressed to his was playing hell with his good intentions, and before he could stop himself, he lowered his mouth to hers. "Throw in a couple dozen brownies—" he brushed her perfect lips with his "—some chocolate-chip-oatmeal cookies—" she parted for him on a soft sigh "—and we'll call it even," he finished as he deepened the kiss.

The combination of Callie's sweet taste and the fact that she was kissing him back sent blood surging through his veins and had his lower body tightening with a need that threatened to buckle his knees. Never in all his thirty-two years had he been aroused as fast or as completely as he was at that very moment.

But when she raised her arms to his neck and tangled her fingers in the hair at his nape, her feather-light touch caused a jolt of hunger to fill every fiber of his being and the need to touch her became overwhelming. Sliding his hand beneath the tail of her T-shirt, when his calloused palm met the satiny skin along her side, his heart thumped hard against his ribs. They'd been so embroiled in their argument over him doing repairs to her house that he hadn't paid attention to the fact that she wasn't wearing a bra.

When he cupped her full breast, then gently slid the pad of his thumb over her tight nipple, her moan of pleasure mingled with his groan of frustration. What the hell did he think he was doing?

Not only was he making out with his flight nurse for God and everybody to see, she was pregnant with another man's child. He wasn't looking for a lasting relationship with any woman. And Callie wasn't a woman who engaged in meaningless flings.

Reluctantly removing his hand from beneath her shirt, he broke the kiss to stare into her wide violet eyes. "Darlin', I think you'd better go back in the house and I'm going to get back to work."

Her porcelain cheeks colored a deep rose and she backed away from him. "I'll be…gone for…a little while," she said, sounding out of breath. "I need to go…to the grocery store."

He frowned. "What for? Your cabinets and freezer are full of food."

She took several steps backward. "I have to see if the store carries fifty-pound bags of flour."

Repositioning his ball cap, Hunter watched her turn and hurry around the side of the house toward the front porch. He'd never seen a woman bake as much as Callie. Maybe it was some kind of hormonal nesting thing.

He shook his head as he grabbed the scraper from the back of the truck and climbed the ladder. Whatever it was, as long as she was inside the house baking and he was outside painting, there wouldn't be any more encounters like the one they'd just shared. And if he repeated it enough times, he just might start to believe it.

When she heard someone knocking on the front door, Callie glanced at the clock on the stove. Hunter couldn't possibly have driven out to the Life Medevac hangar, showered and changed clothes, then driven all the way back to her place in such a short time.

After he'd finished the arduous task of scraping away the peeling paint, he'd told her he was going to go back to the hangar and clean up while she finished dinner. Although she couldn't imagine what it would be, he must have forgotten something.

Wiping her hands on a towel, she checked the pot roast she'd put in the oven earlier, then hurried to open the door. "I'm afraid dinner isn't quite…" Her voice trailed off as icy fear froze her vocal cords and filled every cell in her being.

"Hello, Callie." Craig Culbertson flashed his practiced smile as he brushed past her. "Since you didn't know I was coming for a visit, I didn't expect you to make dinner for me. But I'm sure whatever you're cooking up will be delicious."

"Wh-what are you doing here?" she asked, gripping

the doorknob so hard she wouldn't be surprised if she left her fingerprints embedded in the metal.

"I've missed you." He looked around her small, tidy living room. "What were you thinking when you left Houston for this? It's not even as nice as that minuscule apartment you had."

She ignored his insult and repeated her question. "Why are you here, Craig?"

Turning to face her, his charming smile disappeared; it was replaced with an expression of utter disgust. "Good God! You're pregnant."

Drawing on every ounce of courage she'd ever possessed, she squared her shoulders and placed a protective hand on her stomach. "Yes, I am."

"It's mine, isn't it?" he asked, his tone accusing.

Knowing full well that he wouldn't believe her, she shook her head. "No. The baby belongs to—"

"Me."

Callie had never been so relieved to see anyone in her entire life as she was when Hunter walked through the open door and put his arm around her shoulders. Nor had she ever been as shocked when she heard his claim to be her baby's father.

"This is Craig Culbertson from Houston," she said, silently thanking Hunter for intervening. "Hunter O'Banyon is my—"

"Husband," Hunter interrupted, giving her a look that asked for her to trust him.

"You're married?" Craig shook his head. "You can't be. Your mother said you only moved here a couple of months ago. That's not nearly long enough to find yourself a husband and get knocked up."

"I take exception to the phrase 'knocked up' in reference to my wife's pregnancy," Hunter said, his voice hard as granite.

"Sorry." His tone was anything but apologetic, but Craig apparently decided that Hunter meant business and wasn't one to be trifled with, because he immediately began to backpedal. "It was just an expression, no offense intended."

A fresh wave of fear coursed through Callie as she thought about her last conversation with her mother and how she'd tried to get Callie to tell her who the baby's father was. Had her mother inadvertently hinted to Craig that Callie might be carrying his child?

"Why did you call my mother?" she asked, surprised that her voice was fairly steady considering the state of her nerves.

Craig gave her the smile that she used to think made him look endearingly handsome. Now it only made her feel ill.

"When I discovered your old phone number was no longer in service, I remembered your mother's name, looked up her number and called her to ask how to get in touch with you." He shrugged. "She was reluctant to tell me about your move to Texas until I told her that we'd been seeing each other before you left and how much I missed you. That's when she suggested that if I was ever in the Devil's Fork area that I should look you up. I decided to clear my calendar for the rest of the week and make the drive out here to no-man's-land to see how you're doing."

Callie did a slow burn. She wasn't as angry with her mother as she was with Craig. He'd obviously fed her mother a line about how much he cared, and her mother had fallen for it. Unfortunately Nancy Marshall had never met Craig and had no idea what a snake he was. He wasn't interested in how Callie was doing. His ego was still smarting from the fact that Callie had been the one who'd rejected him instead of the other way around.

"Actually your mother and I talked for some time and I found her to be a very nice lady," Craig added solicitously.

"Oh, really?" Callie shook her head. "It's amazing to me that you carried on a lengthy conversation with my mother when you never would take the time to meet her when you and I were seeing each other."

"You've always been close with your mother, haven't you, Callie?" Craig asked.

She gritted her teeth. "You know I have."

"That's the main reason I find it odd that she didn't know anything about your marriage." He rocked back on his heels as he pointed to Hunter. "It seems to me that she would be the first one you told about your marriage to O'Banyon."

When the timer on the stove went off, indicating that the pot roast was done, Callie reluctantly left the two men standing in her living room glaring at each other. She had no idea what was going to take place or how to deal with it. Hunter's expression from the moment he'd walked through the door had been dark and foreboding. And Craig, as was his usual fashion when he felt threatened, had become arrogant and condescending.

Removing the roast from the oven, she hurried back into the living room before punches started flying. "Craig, I'm sure you have better things to do with your time than stand here debating my marital status."

He shook his head. "Not really. But I will take you up on that offer of dinner."

"I didn't—"

Hunter pulled her to his side and pressed a quick kiss to her lips. "I'm sure we have enough for three, don't we, darlin'?"

Had Hunter lost his mind? The last thing she wanted to do was spend more time in the presence of a snake like Craig Culbertson.

"Well, yes, but—"

"Good." Hunter turned to Craig. "Why don't you have a seat while I help my wife finish getting things on the table?"

Craig gave her a triumphant smile as he plopped down on the end of the love seat. "I think I'll do that."

As soon as she and Hunter entered the kitchen, she turned on him. "What on earth were you thinking?" she demanded, careful to keep her voice low. "I want him out of this house, out of this state and out of my life. For good."

Hunter nodded. "That's the plan."

She looked at him as though he might not be the sharpest knife in the drawer. "And having him stay for dinner is the way to do that?"

"I believe so."

Taking in a deep breath, Hunter still couldn't believe that he'd claimed to be Callie's husband and the father of her baby. But when he'd walked up the porch steps and heard the disgust in Culbertson's voice and the fear in Callie's, Hunter had done the only thing he could think of that didn't involve putting his fist in the man's nose.

"Would you care to explain your reasoning?" she asked as she reached for a pair of oven mitts. "Because I'm having a really hard time understanding."

When he noticed how badly her hands trembled, he took the mitts from her and removed a roasting pan from the oven. Placing it on a hot pad, he tossed the mitts on the counter, then cupped her cheeks with his palms. "The first thing I want you to do is calm down, Callie. I give you my word that as long as I have breath left in my body, I won't let him do anything to harm you or the baby. Is that clear?"

She gazed at him for several long seconds, and the fear he saw in her eyes just about tore him apart. "Yes," she finally said, nodding.

"Good." He reached into the cabinet for a platter. Handing it to her, he explained. "It's clear that Culbertson needs some convincing that you and I are married."

"That came as a surprise to me, too," she said, slicing the roast.

He rubbed the tension building at the back of his neck. "Then it's unanimous, because I was pretty damned shocked about it myself. But it's the only thing I can think of that might make him leave you alone. And that's what you want, isn't it?"

"Absolutely." There wasn't even a heartbeat's hesitation in her voice, and Hunter had no doubt that she didn't want Craig Culbertson anywhere near her.

"The way I see it, if we can convince him how happy we are and how much we're looking forward to our first child, he'll get the message, go back to Houston and you'll never hear from him again." He carried the platter of pot roast over to the small kitchen table while Callie set another place. "Now all we have to do is get a few things straight."

"Like what?"

He removed three glasses from one of the shelves, filled them with ice, then reached for a pitcher of iced tea sitting on the kitchen island. "He'll want to know how we met, when we got married and what we're going to name the baby."

She stared at him openmouthed. "We don't have time to coordinate all that."

Thinking quickly, Hunter said, "Just tell me what you intend to name your son and when you discovered you were pregnant. I'll take care of the rest. Just follow my lead and agree with the line I feed Culbertson."

"This is never going to work," she said, plunking a bowl of mashed potatoes onto the table. "There are too many ways he can trip us up."

Hunter caught her by the shoulders and turned her to face him. "Trust me, Callie. Unless you can think of something else, this is the only way."

He watched her close her eyes, take a deep breath, then opening them, she gave him the information he requested. "You'd better be right about this, Hunter. I won't let him take my baby away from me."

"There's no way in hell, darlin'," he said, giving her a quick hug.

Hunter's heart twisted at the fear he'd heard in her soft voice. He wanted to know what had caused her to be so terrified that Culbertson would try to get custody when the man clearly had no use for children. But that would have to wait until later. Right now they had to con the man into leaving Callie alone for good.

* * *

By the time dinner was over, Callie's nerves were stretched to the breaking point. Sitting between the two men, she'd listened to them discuss everything from baseball player stats to the size of engine they preferred in their vehicles. She wasn't sure whether to be relieved or disappointed that the subject of her and Hunter's marriage had yet to come up.

But that hadn't stopped Hunter from playing his part as the devoted husband to the hilt. Throughout dinner he'd given her smiles that threatened to melt her bones and he'd found every excuse imaginable to touch her. She'd caught Craig taking it all in with great interest, but not once had he asked any of the questions she knew for certain had to be running through his mind.

"Why don't we have dessert in the living room?" Craig asked when Callie rose from her chair to slice pieces of German chocolate cake for them.

"Go ahead and have a seat in there while I help Callie clear the table," Hunter said, rising to gather their plates. "We'll join you in a few minutes."

"It's not going the way we planned," she whispered when Craig left the room.

"Be patient, darlin'." Hunter rinsed the dishes to put in the dishwasher, then measured grounds from one of the canisters for a pot of coffee. "If he doesn't get around to asking, I'll bring up the subject myself."

"I should have never let you talk me into this." She shook her head at her own foolishness. "I'm sure he can see right through this little farce."

"Don't worry. Everything is going to be just fine."

As she allowed Hunter to carry the tray she'd arranged with dessert plates, cups and saucers and a carafe of coffee into the living room, she prayed he was right. Her nerves couldn't stand much more. She already had an almost uncontrollable urge to preheat the oven and start measuring sugar and flour.

"I have a question for you two," Craig said when he placed his empty dessert plate back on the tray. "If you're married, why doesn't Callie wear a wedding band?"

Sitting beside Hunter on the love seat, she had just taken a sip of milk from the glass she'd brought with her from the kitchen and it was all she could do to keep from choking at his blunt question. Panic seized her. She'd been right. Craig knew they were only pretending. Now what were they going to do?

"She had to take her wedding ring off when her fingers started getting a little puffy," Hunter said without missing a beat. He took her left hand in his and brought it to his lips to kiss her ring finger. "Once she has the baby, it will be right back where it belongs."

A wave of tingling heat traveled up her arm, then spread throughout the rest of her body at the loving gesture. She was glad that Hunter had been able to think fast because at the moment she wasn't sure she could think at all.

"When and where did you meet?" Craig asked.

Hunter held up his hand. "See that little scar on my palm? I had to go to the emergency room in Houston when I had a run-in with a fish hook. As soon as I saw Callie, I knew she was the woman for me." Giving her a smile that made her insides feel as if they'd turned to warm pudding, he lightly kissed her cheek. "We were married a few days later and pregnant a few weeks after that."

"Why the rush?" Craig asked, sounding more than a little suspicious.

"Once I see what I want, I don't let it get away from me." Hunter put his arm around her shoulders and held her close to his side. "I'm afraid you're going to have to face facts, Culbertson. She's with me now and I'm not about to let her or our baby go."

Callie watched Craig. She knew him well enough to know that he wasn't entirely convinced. There was a huge hole in their story, and although he hadn't asked again why she'd failed to tell her mother about her marriage to Hunter, Callie knew it was on his mind. But gaining strength from the man holding her so possessively against him, she decided that if the matter came up again, she'd simply tell Craig that she didn't have to explain herself to him or anyone else.

"Well, I suppose I should be going," Craig said as

he rose to his feet. "As always, your cooking was delicious, Callie."

When Hunter stood, then helped her up from her saggy love seat, she began to believe they might have pulled off the ruse. Craig would be leaving town and, with any luck, she'd never have to see or hear from him again.

"Have an enjoyable trip back to Houston," Hunter said as they all walked to the door.

Craig shook his head. "Oh, I'm not leaving the area for several more days. While you two were finishing dinner, I checked the phone book and found a little bed-and-breakfast just up the street." His smirk made Callie want to scream with frustration. "I thought I'd stick around for a while and take in the sights." He laughed as he opened the door. "It's been my experience that you can learn a lot from talking to the locals in a town the size of Devil's Fork."

As Craig walked down the steps and out to his sleek red sports car, Callie felt like crying. How could her life have gotten so out of control in such a short time?

Turning to Hunter, she sighed heavily. "Any more bright ideas?"

He didn't look any happier about the turn of events than she was. "The way I see it, we don't have a whole lot of choice. I'm going to have to move in with you until that sorry excuse for a human being leaves town."

Six

Two hours later, after helping Callie clean up the kitchen, Hunter found himself trying to fold his six-foot-three-inch frame into a comfortable sleeping position on her lumpy love seat. Muttering a word he reserved for extreme situations, he sat up, propped his elbows on his knees and cradled his head in his hands. What the hell had he gotten himself into? And why?

If he'd kept his mouth shut, he'd be sleeping on a fairly comfortable, albeit narrow, bed at the Life Medevac hangar instead of torturing himself on the most uncomfortable piece of furniture known to man. And he for damn sure wouldn't be locked into playing house for the next week with a woman that he was already finding it all but impossible to keep his hands off.

But even as he castigated himself for getting involved, he knew he'd done the right thing. After meeting Culbertson and listening to Callie explain how he and his parents had used their money and influence to take the baby away from the first girl Craig had gotten pregnant, Hunter knew as sure as he knew his own name the Culbertsons wouldn't think twice about trying to do the same thing to Callie.

Shaking his head, Hunter couldn't believe how arrogant they were. What gave them the right to take a baby from his mother simply because Culbertson blood ran through the child's veins? What kind of people thought that it automatically made the mother unfit just because their bank account dwarfed hers?

As he sat there thinking about how ruthless and selfish they were, he realized that if Emerald Larson had wanted to, she could have taken him and his brothers away from their mothers at any time. She certainly had more money and power than the Culbertsons ever dreamed of having and she would have had very little trouble gaining custody of her grandsons.

But instead of viewing the three of them as possessions, Emerald had cared enough to content herself with watching Hunter and his brothers grow up in pictures and P.I. reports in order to ensure they turned out to be as normal and well-adjusted as possible. And for the first time since learning the details of his parentage he began to appreciate the sacrifices that had been made by Emerald on his behalf.

Any lingering traces of anger he still carried from being denied the right to know who his father was dissipated. Although Hunter would always have a problem with any man walking away from a woman when she needed him most, he came to the conclusion that Emerald and her philandering son weren't entirely responsible for the anger and confusion he'd grown up with.

It had been Marlene O'Banyon's choice to agree to Emerald's terms. And although Emerald hadn't required that his mother remain single, Hunter sometimes wondered if she'd signed the confidentiality agreement secretly hoping that one day Owen Larson would come to his senses and return to Miami for her and Hunter. But Owen had never laid eyes on any of his children, nor had he seen their mothers again. And with his death in a boating accident somewhere in the Mediterranean eight months ago, it was never going to happen.

Of course, his mother had no idea that old Owen had sown more than just one wild oat. Although she was the first woman he'd gotten pregnant, she certainly hadn't been the last. Hell, Hunter doubted that Emerald was completely certain that he, Nick and Caleb were Owen's only offspring.

But that was immaterial now. The fact of the matter was, in light of the way the Culbertsons had dealt with a similar situation, he understood and could even commend his grandmother for handling everything the way she had.

Lost in thought, it took a moment for Hunter to realize that Callie had gotten out of bed and was tip-toeing her way through the living room into the kitchen. "Can't sleep?" he asked, careful to keep his voice nonthreatening so as not to frighten her.

Her startled cry was loud enough to wake the dead. So much for trying not to frighten her.

"It's just me, Callie."

"Dear heavens, you scared me out of a year's growth," she said, clutching something to the front of her robe.

"I'm sorry." He switched on the lamp at the end of the love seat. "I didn't mean to…" He stopped to stare at her when he realized what she was carrying. "What the hell are you doing with your apron at—" he checked his watch "—midnight?"

"I'm too keyed up to sleep," she said defensively. "I thought I'd find something to do."

He frowned. "So you're going to start cooking?"

She breezed past him to enter the kitchen. "Every-one deals with stress in their own way. Some people drink. Some eat. I bake."

That explained why she'd made enough baked goods to stock a chain of grocery stores, he thought as he followed her. She'd been scared witless since learning she was pregnant that Culbertson would find out about the baby. Now that he had, it appeared that Callie would be making enough cookies to feed every man, woman and child in the whole damned state.

"Our shift starts in a little less than eighteen hours." He yawned. "Don't you think it would be a good idea to be well rested when we go to work?"

She shook her head as she reached for a set of measuring cups and the canister of flour. "Don't worry about me, I'll be fine. You're the one who needs rest to pilot the helicopter. Go back into the living room and get some sleep."

"That's easier said than done," he muttered.

"I promise I won't make much noise," she said, knocking over the cup of flour she'd just measured.

"That's not the problem." He pulled out a chair and sat down at the table. "I'm too tall."

"Excuse me?"

She looked thoroughly confused and so darned cute standing there in her nightclothes and apron, he had to force himself to remember what they were talking about. "The love seat is roughly fifty inches long and I'm six foot three. You do the math."

Her eyes widened. "Oh, dear. I'm sorry. I hadn't thought of it being too short for you." She shook her head. "But it's not a problem. You can take my bed and I'll sleep on the love seat."

"Like hell." He wasn't about to sleep on a comfortable bed while she endured that instrument of torture in her condition.

"Why not?" she asked as she cleaned up the flour she'd spilled. "I'm at least ten inches shorter and shouldn't have nearly as much trouble getting comfortable."

"You're pregnant."

"And you're bossy." She grinned. "But I'm trying not to hold that against you."

Her pretty smile sent a wave of heat straight through him, and he could think of several things he'd like for her to hold against him—every one of them soft, warm and deliciously feminine. He swallowed hard. Thinking along those lines could only accomplish one of two things. It would either get him in a whole lot deeper than he was comfortable with or drive him completely insane. And he wasn't altogether sure that he hadn't already crossed the line in both areas.

"I can sleep in one of the chairs and—"

"Wake up with a terribly stiff neck," she interrupted, dropping an egg on the counter. "Darn." Grabbing a paper towel, she cleaned up the mess. "If I'm going to be flying with you, I not only want you well rested, I'd like for you to have your full range of motion."

"I can manage in the chair." He stood up and started toward the living room, but her soft hand on his back stopped him dead in his tracks and sent a jolt of electric current throughout his system.

"I think we're overlooking the obvious here," she said, turning to measure more flour into a bowl. "I'll probably be up for hours before I'm relaxed enough to go to sleep. There's no reason for you to be uncomfortable when there's an empty bed that you could be sleeping in. And if I want to go to sleep before you get up, I'll be careful not to wake you when I lie down."

She had a point. It was pretty silly for him to try to sleep in the chair when he could be stretched out. But just knowing that she'd eventually be getting in bed with him was enough to send him into orbit.

"I guess that could work," he said, thinking aloud. "And we're both adults. There's no reason we can't handle this." And maybe if he repeated it enough, he'd start to believe it.

"Exactly." She waved her hand toward the other room as she reached for a spoon and promptly knocked over a container of baking powder. "You're distracting me. Now go to bed and let me get started on these cookies."

Yawning, he scratched his bare chest and headed for her bedroom. Hopefully he'd be out like a light as soon as his head hit the pillow. And if he believed that, he was sure somebody had a piece of beachfront property in the middle of Arizona that he'd be fool enough to buy.

* * *

A couple of hours after Hunter went to lie down in her bed, Callie turned off the light in the kitchen and quietly walked into the bedroom. Making several dozen cookies had helped, but her nerves were still on edge and she expected they would remain that way until she was certain Craig was out of her life for good.

As she removed her slippers, then turned to pull back the cover, she forgot all about her current problem with Craig and focused on the sight of Hunter's broad back. From the muted moonlight filtering into the room through the sheer drapes she could see that he was lying on his stomach with the sheet covering him from the waist down.

Her heart stalled and she swallowed hard as the sight of all that delicious masculine skin reminded her of earlier in the kitchen when she'd first seen his bare chest. The play of his perfectly defined chest muscles beneath a light sprinkling of dark hair had fascinated her beyond words and distracted her to the point she'd been about as coordinated as a bull in a china shop.

How on earth was she going to be able to sleep with all that raw masculinity mere inches away? And why did her double bed suddenly seem as though it had shrunk to the size of a cot?

Wishing she had bought a two-bedroom house instead of a charming one-bedroom cottage, she shook her head as she jammed her feet back in her slippers.

She'd go into the kitchen, grab a handful of chocolate chips and lie down on the love seat.

"Are you going to stand there the rest of the night or are you going to get into bed?"

She jumped at the sound of Hunter's voice and her cheeks heated with embarrassment at being caught staring at him. Thank heavens there wasn't enough light in the room for him to see her guilty expression. "I…didn't want to…disturb you."

He rolled to his back and gazed up at her. "I wasn't asleep."

"What's wrong?" The way he'd been yawning before he'd gone to bed, she'd have thought he'd be asleep before he had a chance to close his eyes. "Is the mattress too soft for you?"

"No, it's quite comfortable."

She frowned as she gingerly sat down on the side of the bed. "Then what's the problem?"

"I've been thinking—"

"I'm not altogether sure I want to hear this," she interrupted warily. "The last time you shared your thoughts is what got us into this mess."

"Are you going to take off your robe and lie down?"

She swallowed hard. It would have been hard enough to stretch out beside him if he'd been asleep. But awake? Just the thought caused a tingling sensation to skip over every cell in her body.

"That's what you've been thinking about?"

"No." His deep chuckle sent a shiver straight up her spine. "But you've been going on adrenaline all evening, and I think it would probably be a good idea for the baby's sake if you tried to relax."

Callie knew he was right. But she wasn't sure that was going to be an option, especially with him so close.

"Are you going to keep me guessing or are you going to tell me what you've come up with this time?" she hedged.

He shook his head. "Not until you lie down."

Exasperated beyond words, she shook her head. "I think it would be best if I slept on the love seat."

"Why? You aren't afraid of sleeping in the same bed with me, are you?" She couldn't see much of his expression in the darkened room, but she'd heard the laughter and good-natured challenge in his voice.

"Don't be silly," she lied. "I just think since we're clearly attracted to each other, it might not be a good idea."

"Remember, we're both adults," he said softly. "I give you my word that nothing is going to happen that you don't want to happen."

It shouldn't be a problem, she told herself as she stood up to remove her robe. She wasn't sure why, but she trusted him. And she knew for certain she didn't have to worry about herself. The last thing she wanted or needed was to become involved with another man.

When she slipped into bed, he turned to his side,

propped his elbow on the pillow and rested his head against her palm. His proximity sent a delicious little thrill from the top of her head all the way to the tips of her toes. She did her best to ignore it.

"I think we should get married."

His voice was low and intimate, and it took a moment for her to realize what he'd said. When she did, her heart slammed against her ribs.

"You can't be serious."

When she started to get out of bed, his hand on her arm stopped her. "Think about it, darlin'. It won't take much effort on Culbertson's part to discover that we aren't married or that I've never been to Houston."

"And this just occurred to you?" She rubbed at her suddenly throbbing temples. "Why did I let you talk me into this? I told you it wouldn't work."

"That's why I'm suggesting we get married," he said patiently. "It doesn't matter when we got married, we'll still be husband and wife."

"I can't see where that would do anything but add one more complication to an already impossible situation." A sudden thought caused a chill to race through her, and she had to take a deep breath in order to get words passed the tightness in her throat. "He could ask for a DNA test to prove paternity."

"He might, but something tells me he won't."

Her breath caught on a soft sob. If he and his parents learned that her son had been fathered by Craig, the

Culbertsons were the kind of people who would intervene and take her baby away from her—not because they loved the child, but because they viewed him as one of their possessions. They'd find an excuse to find her unworthy or unfit to raise their heir, the same as they'd done that poor girl twelve years ago.

"There's no way out of…this." A chill ran the length of her spine. "They're going to take my child away from me and there's nothing I can do to stop them."

Hunter reached out to wrap his strong arms around her and cradle her to him. "Not as long as I'm around to stop them, they won't."

"I can't see how—"

"Taking a child away from a single parent isn't as difficult as it is from a married couple."

"Yes, but the Culbertsons are quite wealthy and can hire the best lawyers. And I'm sure they'll see that the case is heard by a judge who travels in the same social circle they do." She placed her hand over her stomach. "We'd be fighting a losing battle."

"Let them hire whoever they want or get whatever judge they think will go along with their request." He kissed her forehead. "It's not like I don't have a few connections of my own."

Pulling back to look at him, she shook her head. "I'm not sure who you think you know, but it's going to take more than a connection or two to keep them from taking my son."

"You might be surprised." He gently brushed a strand of hair from her cheek with his index finger. "Let me worry about dealing with the Culbertsons and their lawyers. I'm going to do some checking, but I suspect there's more to his visit than what he's saying."

Anger and frustration filled her. "This is the very reason I detest rich people. They think that because they have money it gives them the right to do anything they please."

"Not all people of means are like the Culbertsons, Callie," he said quietly. "My father's family had money, but there was never a threat of them taking me or my brothers away from our mothers."

Remembering their conversation on the trip back from El Paso, Callie bit her lower lip to keep it from trembling as a fresh wave of fear coursed through her. "I'd say your father's family is the exception, not the rule."

"Maybe, but I'm betting it's closer to being the other way around." He lightly ran his palm up and down her arm, sending a wave of tingling warmth to every part of her. "At any rate, I promise you have nothing to fear from the Culbertsons as long as I'm around."

"I hope you're right," she said, hiding a yawn behind her hand.

He kissed the top of her head. "We'll talk more in the morning. Right now we both need to get some rest."

Within moments his deep, even breathing signaled that Hunter had fallen asleep. But, as tired as she was, Callie couldn't stop thinking about the threat that Craig posed or Hunter's offer of marriage.

Everything he said made perfect sense and could very well solve her problem. But friendship only went so far. She couldn't believe he was willing to enter into something as serious as marriage simply to help her. What did he expect to get out of it for himself? And what would happen if they were successful in keeping the Culbertsons from taking her baby away from her? How long before Hunter asked for an annulment or a divorce?

Thoroughly exhausted from the tension of Craig's unexpected visit and the speculation of what would happen if she did go along with Hunter's insane suggestion, Callie felt herself begin to drift off to sleep. But instead of having nightmares of her baby being taken away from her by Craig and his family, she dreamed of marriage to a tall, dark-haired, handsome man with a sexy-as-sin voice and devastating kisses.

The feel of thin, downy-soft hair against her cheek, the steady beat of a heart beneath her ear and the scent of clean masculine skin assailed Callie's senses as she floated in the surreal world between sleep and wakefulness. When a pair of strong arms tightened around her, she smiled and snuggled against the hard male body beside her.

"Good morning, sleepyhead."

The sound of Hunter's voice caused her eyes to fly open and had her tilting her head to meet his incredible green gaze. She was lying with her head pillowed on his broad chest and her arm thrown over his flat belly. But it was the realization that her leg was draped over his muscular thigh—his bare muscular thigh—that sent a shiver of excitement up her spine and had her wondering if she'd be able to draw her next breath.

"H-how long have you been awake?"

"About an hour."

Goose bumps shimmered over her skin at the vibration of his rich baritone rumbling up from deep in his chest. But it was the feel of his hard arousal straining at his briefs that had her gingerly moving her leg away from his. They were treading in dangerous territory and it would definitely be best to put some distance between them.

"Where are you going?" His warm breath stirred the fine hair at her temple and caused her heart to skip several beats.

"I, um, should probably get up and cook something for breakfast."

He held her firmly against him when she tried to pull from his arms. "I've got a hunger, but it's not for food."

A delightful heat like nothing she'd ever known began to flow through her veins at his candid comment.

"I—it wouldn't be a good idea to complicate things more than they already are."

His deep chuckle caused the warmth inside of her to pool in the pit of her belly. "Darlin', kissing isn't complicated." He brushed her lips with his, sending a delightful tingling sensation all the way to her toes. "It's one of the purest forms of pleasure a man and woman can share."

The sound of his voice, his provocative words and the feel of his calloused palm caressing her side through her thin cotton gown were like a drug and she suddenly had a hard time remembering her own name, let alone why it would make their current situation more difficult. But she ceased thinking at all when his mouth settled over hers and he tenderly traced the outline of her lips with his tongue.

"This is…insane," she murmured, trying to draw some much-needed air into her lungs.

He nibbled kisses along her jawline to the sensitive hollow below her ear. "Do you want me to stop?"

"I should demand that you stop and get out of my house immediately."

His lips blazed a trail down her neck to her collarbone. "But you aren't going to do that?"

With a myriad of delightful sensations coursing through her, she had to concentrate on his question. "N-no."

"Why not?" he asked as he ran his palm back down

her side, then slipped his hand beneath the hem of her gown.

His fingers sliding along her bare skin made breathing all but impossible and caused the heat in her lower belly to intensify. "Wh-what you're doing…feels too good."

"Do you want me to stop?"

Unable to think clearly, she shook her head. "Don't you dare."

He caressed her hip, then her ribs as he slowly moved his hand up her body. "Are you aware of what's going to happen if I continue?"

When he covered her breast with his hand, then chafed her puckered nipple with the pad of his thumb, need coursed through her to settle deep in the most feminine part of her. "W-we'll make love."

His hand continued to caress her overly sensitized skin. "Is that what you want, Callie?"

Staring into his dark green eyes, her heart pounded hard in her chest. From the moment they'd first met there had been a magnetic pull drawing them together, a chemistry they'd both tried but found impossible to deny. And with each kiss the tension between them had heightened until it had become a force that was impossible for either of them to fight.

Whether it was her pregnancy hormones that caused a desire stronger than anything she'd ever known or something more, she didn't want him to stop. She wanted to feel the warmth of Hunter's kisses and the passion of his loving touch.

"It's pure insanity. But yes, I want to make love with you, Hunter."

Seven

At Callie's admittance that she wanted to make love with him, Hunter's heart slammed against his rib cage so hard he was surprised it hadn't jumped right out of his chest. Throughout the night he'd lain with her in his arms, and with each tick of the clock her soft body and sweet womanly scent had increased the tension he'd been fighting from the moment he'd laid eyes on her. But when she'd awakened and stared up at him with her sexy violet eyes, he'd become harder than he'd ever been in his life and could no more have stopped himself from tasting and touching her than he could stop the sun from rising in the east each morning.

But as much as he wanted to sink himself deep inside of her, to hear her call his name as he pleasured her, he couldn't bear the thought that she might regret one minute of what they would share. "Are you sure that making love is what you really want, Callie?"

His heart stalled and he found himself holding his breath when she closed her eyes and remained silent for several long seconds. Then, to his relief, she opened her eyes and nodded her head.

"I think I'll go into total meltdown if we don't."

Taking a deep breath, he tried to slow the liquid fire racing through his veins. "I know I should have asked this before things went this far, but would your doctor be okay with our making love?"

Her porcelain cheeks colored a pretty pink as she nodded. "The obstetrician has given me the go-ahead for normal activity with no restrictions. And that includes lovemaking."

Hunter couldn't believe the level of relief that washed over him. If she'd told him there was even the slightest possibility of a problem or the tiniest bit of discomfort for her, he'd have found some way—no matter how difficult—to walk away. But knowing there was nothing to prevent them from having a pleasurable and satisfying experience sent a fresh wave of heat straight to his groin.

Unfortunately it was short-lived. He hadn't planned on spending the night with Callie, let alone making love with her, and protection hadn't even crossed his mind when he'd left the hangar yesterday evening. But he was thinking about it now. Or, more accurately, the lack of it.

But as he gazed at the woman in his arms, he realized there was no possibility of him making her pregnant. And truth to tell, it wouldn't matter to him if she wasn't already expecting a child.

The thought of Callie carrying his baby appealed to him more than he could have ever imagined and should have scared the living hell out of him. It was something he didn't understand, wasn't entirely comfortable with and, at the moment, didn't intend to analyze. All that mattered was bringing her pleasure, cherishing her as she was meant to be cherished.

Without a moment's hesitation he gathered her close and covered her mouth with his. Her soft lips molded to his with a hungry desperation that matched his own and sent fire racing through his veins with the swiftness of a raging river.

When she parted for him to deepen the kiss, Hunter thought his head might come right off his shoulders as she boldly stroked his tongue with hers and engaged him in an erotic game of advance and retreat. She was letting him know that she felt the passion as deeply as he did, that she wanted him as much as he wanted her.

Breaking the kiss, he nibbled his way to the base of her throat as he reached for the hem of her gown.

"Lift your hips, darlin'," he whispered against her satiny skin.

When he'd whisked away her panties and thin cotton gown, he quickly removed his boxer briefs, then tossing the garments to the floor beside the bed, gathered her back into his arms. At the feel of her satiny skin against him, desire raced through his veins, and he had to fight an almost uncontrollable urge to cover her with his body and sink himself deep inside of her.

His entire being pulsed with the urgent need to claim her, but he was determined not to rush things no matter what his body demanded. "You feel so soft...." He trailed kisses down the base of her throat, then past her collarbone to the slope of her breast. "So sweet."

As he teased her with a light swirling motion, the fire of need in his belly grew when she threaded her fingers in his hair and pulled him closer. Arching her back, she gave him better access to the hardened tip, and taking her into his mouth, he chafed her with his tongue and caressed her with his lips.

"P-please, Hunter."

"Not yet, darlin'." Moving his hand down her side to her hip and beyond, he cupped her at the apex of her thighs. "I want to make sure you're ready for me."

"If I was any more ready...I'd burn to a crisp." Her voice sounded wispy and breathless and he had no doubt she was as turned-on as he was.

Parting her, he stroked her, then touched her intimately. Her moist warmth and moan of pleasure assured him that she needed him as much as he needed her.

"I want you to promise me something," he said as he continued to stroke her.

"Anything." He watched her close her eyes and catch her lower lip between her teeth a moment before she whimpered, "You're driving me…crazy."

Her response to his touch heightened his own passion, and he had to take several deep breaths in order to force himself to slow down. "I want you to promise me that if there's even the slightest bit of discomfort, you'll tell me."

"I promise." When she opened her eyes to gaze up at him, the desire in the violet depths robbed him of breath. "Please…make love to me, Hunter."

Unable to deny either one of them any longer, he nudged her knees apart and levered himself over her. As he moved his lower body into position, he settled his mouth over hers at the same time he pressed himself forward.

Slowly, carefully, he pushed into her, and the feel of her tight body melting around him as he sank deeper and deeper had him clenching his teeth as he struggled for control. But when she raised her hips for more of him, the slender thread of his restraint snapped and he buried himself completely within her feminine depths.

With every muscle in his body taut with the need to complete the act of loving her, Hunter forced himself to remain completely still. She needed time to adjust to him and he needed time to savor the feeling of being completely one with the most desirable woman he'd ever known.

Gathering her close, he kissed her sweet lips. "I'm going to try to go slow, but I want you so damned much I'm not sure that's an option."

Her smile caused the fire threatening to consume him to flare out of control. "I want you just as much."

He held her gaze with his as he eased his hips back then forward, thrusting into her again and again. As he felt her respond by meeting him halfway, he increased the rhythm with each stroke, and in no time he felt her body tighten around his, signaling that she was poised to find her release.

When she wrapped her legs around his waist to hold him close, the pressure in his body increased tenfold and it was all he could do to hold himself in check. But he wasn't going to find his satisfaction without her, and sliding his hand between them, he touched her as he thrust into her one last time.

Her moan of pleasure and the quivering of her tiny inner muscles rippling around him as she found her satisfaction triggered his own completion. Heat and light flashed behind his tightly closed eyes as he surrendered to the storm, and feeling as if his world had been reduced to just the two of them, he emptied himself deep inside of her.

As Hunter slowly drifted back to reality, an emotion filled his chest that he didn't dare put a name to. He'd never experienced anything as amazing as what he'd just shared with Callie. Her passionate response to his touch had excited him in ways he'd only dreamed of and he felt more alive than he had in years.

"Are you all right?" he asked when he finally found the strength to move to her side.

"I-I'm fine."

A slight crack in her voice had him rising up to look down at her beautiful face. The tears he saw welling up in her eyes scared him as little else could. If he'd hurt her in any way, he'd never forgive himself.

"Callie, darlin', what's wrong?"

"Nothing. Making love with you was one of the most beautiful experiences I've ever had." She cupped his cheek with her palm, and her smile lit the darkest corners of his soul. "Thank you."

Weak with relief, he shook his head. "I should be thanking you. You were incredible."

When she hid a yawn behind her delicate hand, he kissed the top of her head. "You were up pretty late and it's still early. Why don't we take a nap, then we can talk over breakfast." He hadn't much more than gotten the words out before her shallow breathing signaled that she'd drifted off to sleep.

As he watched the predawn shadows in the room melt away with the light of day, Hunter held Callie close and thought about what they would be talking about later. After the accident and Ellen's death, he'd never intended to ask another woman to marry him. But these were a different set of circumstances. He and Callie wouldn't be marrying for love. They would be doing the only thing he could think of that might discourage Craig Culbertson from trying to take her baby away from her.

He closed his eyes and tried to think of some other way to help Callie. From the time he'd gone to bed until she'd entered the bedroom a couple of hours later, all he'd been able to think about was how they could stop Culbertson and his family.

Hunter had no idea what the man's motive was, but he must have learned about Callie's pregnancy from her mother and shown up to confirm his suspicions that he was the father. Considering the disgust in his voice when he'd accusingly asked her if the child was his, Hunter was surprised that Culbertson hadn't jumped at the chance for someone else to take responsibility. But he hadn't, and Hunter had every intention of pulling out all the stops to find out why. And he knew exactly who to contact to help him start making inquiries into the matter. He'd get the name of a discreet private investigator from Emerald's trusted assistant, Luther Freemont, and see what they could dig up on Culbertson.

If he'd wanted to, Hunter could have asked outright for Emerald to intervene on Callie's behalf and he had no doubt that she would have. But that wasn't his style. Whether it was pride or bullheaded stubbornness, he fought his own battles. He'd offered to help Callie and he'd be the one to see the matter through to the end.

Another reason he didn't want to get Emerald involved was that he wasn't ready for anyone—and especially Callie—at Life Medevac to learn of his relationship to the indomitable Mrs. Larson. For one thing, he had yet to prove himself with the business she'd given him to run. And for another, Callie had trust issues with anyone who had money. If she were to discover that he was Emerald Larson's grandson and had been given a trust fund large enough to make a dent in the national debt, as well as being in line to inherit part of Emerald Inc., she'd automatically assume he was like the Culbertsons and refuse his help. And that was something they both knew she couldn't afford to do.

Gazing down at her sleeping so peacefully in his arms, he fleetingly wondered if getting married would pose a threat to either of their hearts. But he immediately dismissed the concern. They wouldn't be marrying for love, and as long as they kept things in perspective and their emotions in check, there shouldn't be a problem for either of them.

Satisfied that he had everything under control,

Hunter relaxed and closed his eyes. They'd stay together as long as it took to settle this business with Culbertson once and for all, then evaluate the best way to handle the dissolution of their marriage.

An unexpected twinge of regret tightened his chest at the thought, but he ignored it. He and Callie were friends now and they would remain friends once they parted ways. And that's just the way it had to stay.

"Where's your husband, Callie?"

Callie went perfectly still at the sound of the familiar voice. Needing a refill on her prenatal vitamins, she'd stopped at the drugstore on her way to start her shift at Life Medevac. She didn't have the time nor the desire to deal with the likes of Craig Culbertson.

"Not that it's any of your business, but Hunter owns the air-ambulance service and had some paperwork to deal with," she said, heading back to her car.

She could pick up the vitamins another time. Right now she wanted nothing more than to put as much distance between her and Craig as humanly possible.

But before she could get the driver's door open, he caught her by the arm. "What's your hurry? Surely you have enough time to talk to an old friend."

Extricating herself from his grasp, she turned to face him. "We aren't friends and never will be. Now if you'll excuse me, I need to get to work."

His knowing smirk was enough to make her want

to scream. "If your husband owns the business, going in late shouldn't be a problem for you."

She reached for the handle on her car door. "I need to be there on time to relieve the on-duty crew."

He shook his head as he placed his hand on the driver's door to hold it shut. "What you need to do is answer a few questions."

"No, I don't."

"Oh, I think you do." He reached out to trace his index finger down her cheek. "It seems that none of the people here in town knew anything about you and O'Banyon being married. In fact, Mr. Jones over at the grocery store was quite surprised to hear the news."

A cold chill slithered up her spine at Craig's touch. She must have had blinders on not see that his charm was a weapon, not an endearing quality. How could she have ever found herself attracted to such a reptile?

Batting his hand away, she shook her head. "Don't ever touch me again."

"You used to like for me to touch you, Callie," he said, trying to affect an injured look.

"That's ancient history." She tried to remove his hand where he held the car door. "All I want from you now is to be left alone."

His eyes narrowed and a sneer replaced his wounded expression. "Now is that any way to talk to your baby's daddy?"

"Just because you can fertilize an egg doesn't make

you father material. That takes someone special." She jerked the car door from his grasp and started to get in. "Someone who is actually capable of loving a child."

"Like O'Banyon?"

"Yes. Exactly like Hunter."

His sarcastic laugh caused her to clench her fists until her knuckles ached. "Why don't you give up the charade, Callie? We both know you're no more married than I am. If you come back to Houston now, maybe I'll forget that you and O'Banyon tried to dupe me into believing the baby belongs to him." He shrugged. "Who knows? I might even be persuaded to let you have visitation rights."

Fear so strong it threatened to the buckle her knees ran through her. "As long as I have breath left in my body, you won't take my child away from me," she said, doing her best to keep her voice steady.

His knowing smile made her skin crawl. "That remains to be seen, my dear."

As Callie got into the car, her hands shook so badly that it took a couple of tries before she was able to fit her key into the ignition. Everything she'd feared for the past several months was coming true.

As she backed the car from the parking space and drove the short distance to the Life Medevac hangar outside of town, her body trembled and tears ran un-checked down her cheeks. For reasons she didn't have time nor the inclination to analyze, all she could think of was getting to Hunter. She knew it made no sense at all considering the short time they'd known each other, but with him she felt more secure than she had in her entire life. And although she hated being vulnerable and dependent in any way, his reassuring presence gave her strength.

Parking her car at the side of the hangar, she hurried into the dispatch room. Thankfully the on-duty crew and Mary Lou were occupied with a game of Texas Hold 'Em poker. She knew she looked more than a little upset and she didn't particularly want to endure a barrage of questions from Mary Lou.

"Is Hunter in his office?" she asked as she breezed past them.

"He's been in there all afternoon making phone calls," Mary Lou answered without looking up from her cards.

When Callie came to Hunter's office, she didn't even hesitate as she opened the door and walked into the room. Craig might think he had the upper hand, but she wasn't going to stand by and let him take her son away without a fight. And if that meant entering into a marriage with a man she barely knew, then that's exactly what she was going to do.

"If you're still willing to marry me, my answer is yes."

Eight

Hunter was on his feet and rounding the desk in a flash. Callie looked as if she'd seen a ghost, and the tears streaming down her cheeks just about tore him apart.

"What's happened?"

When he took her into his arms, she burrowed into his embrace. As she told him about meeting up with Culbertson and the man's arrogant attitude, pure fury burned at Hunter's gut.

"Do you honestly think we would have a chance of stopping him if we were married?" she asked, trembling against him.

"There's not a doubt in my mind, darlin'."

If he could have gotten his hands on Culbertson at

that very moment, Hunter would have choked the life out of him for putting her through that. The man was without question the sorriest excuse for a human being he'd ever had the misfortune to meet, and it was going to give him great pleasure to deal the arrogant jerk a good dose of reality.

Hunter had spent the entire afternoon on the phone with Emerald's personal assistant, Luther Freemont, and the private investigator Emerald Inc. hired for running background checks on potential employees for Emerald's various companies. After speaking with the man at length, Hunter was confident that if there was anything they could use to combat Culbertson's attempt to gain custody of Callie's baby, the P.I. would find it.

And on the outside chance that Culbertson was squeaky-clean—which Hunter knew damned good and well he wasn't—he and Callie would establish themselves as a married couple with a stable home life that no lawyer, judge or social worker could argue wasn't perfect for raising a child.

"I don't want you spending any more time worrying about Culbertson or what he's going to do," Hunter said as he soothingly rubbed at the tension along her spine.

She leaned back to look at him, and the anxiety he saw in the depths of her expressive eyes caused his gut to twist into a tight knot. "Th-that's easier said than done."

"Do you trust me, Callie?"

"Yes." There wasn't so much as a hint of uncertainty in her answer.

"I give you my word that everything is going to work out." He gave her a reassuring smile. "By the time this is settled, Craig Culbertson will be running back to Houston like a tail-tucked dog."

"I hope you're right."

"I am."

He sealed his promise with a kiss, and by the time he raised his head, his body was as hard as a chunk of granite. Taking a deep breath, he rested his forehead against hers. He had no idea how she'd managed to get under his skin so quickly, but there was no denying that he found her to be the most exciting woman he'd had the good fortune to meet in the past five years. And the thought of making love to her every night, then holding her as she slept, was enough to send a laser of heat straight through him.

"Why…are you willing…to do this for me, Hunter?" she asked, every bit as breathless as he was. "What's in this for you?"

He'd asked himself the same question at least a dozen times and the answer had been surprisingly simple. "Even though my father's family is well off, my grandmother felt that my brothers and I would be much better off being raised by loving mothers who taught us a solid set of values, instead of giving us everything we wanted, like she'd given our father." He grinned. "Her logic must have worked, because we all turned out to be well-adjusted and productive, instead of selfish and hopelessly irresponsible like her son."

"Your grandmother must be a very special, very wise lady."

"She's definitely one of a kind," he said evasively, thinking that was an understatement. "But the point is, I believe every kid deserves the same chance she gave me and my brothers."

"In other words, you're doing this for the sake of my son?"

Hunter nodded. "I know you'll be a great mom and raise him with the love and guidance he needs. He wouldn't get that from Culbertson and his family."

She shook her head disapprovingly. "He'd turn out to be just like Craig—hedonistic, selfish and shallow."

"Exactly." Hunter kissed her forehead. "And to answer your second question, the only thing I expect to get out of our marriage is the satisfaction of knowing that I stopped that from happening."

"How long—"

Placing his finger to her lips, he shook his head. "Let's take it one day at a time. After we take care of this business with Culbertson, then we'll discuss how we want to handle…things." He had no idea why, but he couldn't bring himself to say the word *annulment* or *divorce*.

He watched her nibble on her lower lip as she gazed

at him for several seconds. "Does that mean you'll be moving in with me for a while?"

"Husbands and wives usually live together, darlin'." He grinned. "Of course, you could always move into my room here at the hangar."

For the first time since walking into the room she smiled. "I don't think that would work very well considering you have a twin-size bed."

"Oh, I think it might work out real well." Sharing any bed with Callie sounded good to him. He brushed her lips with his. "When we aren't making love, I can hold you close while we sleep."

He watched a spark of awareness replace the worry in her violet eyes. "That might work for a time. But what happens when my tummy is as big as an overinflated balloon?"

"Good point," he said, wondering what it would feel like to have her baby moving under his hands. A sharp pang of regret that he'd never feel his own child move inside her knifed through him, but he did his best to ignore it. Suddenly feeling as if he might be drowning, he added, "Maybe your bed would be best."

"When do you want to do this?"

He laughed, relieving some of his tension. "If it had been left up to me, we wouldn't have gotten out of bed this morning."

Her cheeks coloring a pretty pink fascinated the

hell out of him. "I meant, when do you think we should get married?"

"I know." He gave her a quick kiss, then stepped back before he gave in to temptation and took her down the hall to test out his narrow bed. "How does tomorrow afternoon sound?"

"Impossible." The sound of laughter in her sweet voice was like a balm to his soul. "Besides the fact that we'll be on duty, there's a three-day waiting period in the state of Texas from the time we obtain a license until we get married."

"I happen to know there isn't a waiting period in New Mexico." He took her by the hand and led her over to the door. "And remember, I'm the boss. I can have the Evac II crew come in on standby for the day while you and I make a trip up to Carlsbad."

She looked a little dazed as they walked out into the hall. "This is all happening so fast."

"Things will slow down after tomorrow." He put his arm around her slender shoulders and held her to his side. "Now put on your best smile, darlin'. We have an announcement to make to our coworkers."

"Do you, Calantha Marshall, take this man to be your lawful wedded husband? To have and to hold…"

The rotund judge droned on, but Callie had no idea if he recited the words of the traditional wedding ceremony or if he was trying to auction off a pile of dirt.

She was way too nervous to think of anything but the fact that she'd not only let Hunter talk her into marrying him, they were actually going through with it.

When the Honorable Juan Ricardo cleared his throat and looked at her expectantly, she swallowed hard and forced herself to concentrate on what he'd asked. "I do," she said, surprised that her voice sounded fairly steady considering the state of her nerves.

Judge Ricardo nodded his approval, then turned to Hunter and asked the same question.

Giving her a smile that curled her toes inside her cross trainers, Hunter's voice was strong and sure when he answered. "I do."

"Do you have a ring?" the judge asked, giving Hunter an expectant look.

Callie's cheeks heated as Hunter shook his head. They were probably the most ill-prepared couple to be getting married that the judge had ever seen.

"As soon as she said she'd marry me, I didn't want to take the time to pick out a ring," Hunter said, giving the man a conspiratorial grin. "I was afraid she might change her mind."

Judge Ricardo chuckled. "Then, by the power vested in me by the state of New Mexico, I pronounce you husband and wife. You can kiss your bride, son."

When Hunter took her into his arms to seal their union, his kiss caused her head to spin and her knees to feel as if they were made of rubber. Raising his head, he gazed at her for several long seconds before he turned and thanked the judge, then took her hand in his and led her out of the courthouse.

As they got into the Life Medevac truck for the drive back to Devil's Fork, she still couldn't believe how quickly everything had taken place. "What in heaven's name have we done?"

When he reached out and covered her hand with his, a sense of well-being coursed through her. It was completely unexpected and caused her to catch her breath. Dear heavens, was her attraction to Hunter more than a case of overactive prenatal hormones?

Being a registered nurse, she knew that due to an imbalance in hormone levels, during the second trimester some expectant mothers felt more sensual and sexy than they'd ever felt in their lives. She'd naturally assumed that was the reason she'd given in to desire and passion when she'd made love with Hunter. But now? Could she actually be falling for him?

No, that wasn't possible. She'd only known him a short time, and although her attraction to him was stronger than anything she'd ever felt, that didn't mean she loved him.

"You're awfully quiet," he said, bringing her hand to his lips to kiss the back of it.

Thinking quickly, she smiled. "I was contemplating whether to keep my last name, hyphenate it or change it to yours."

He nodded. "I did an Internet search this morning and found a Web site with a list of things that a bride needs to do after the wedding. Changing her personal documents and identification was on the list." He gave her a seductive smile. "It's up to you, darlin'. But I think Callie Marshall-O'Banyon or just Callie O'Banyon sounds pretty good."

"Since our marriage is only temporary, I suppose it would make more sense to hyphenate."

"Then Callie Marshall-O'Banyon it is."

"For now."

"Right. For now."

As they rode in relative silence on the way back to Devil's Fork, Callie couldn't help but wonder why the thought that her name change wasn't going to be permanent caused her to feel a deep sadness. She'd known up front that they were only getting married in order to thwart Craig's efforts to take her baby away from her. So why was she feeling so darned melancholy?

But as she analyzed her reaction, she supposed it was only natural to feel a bit depressed. She'd always thought that once she got married and took her husband's name it would be for the rest of her life. Of course, that had been when she'd been idealistic and thought the only reason she would ever marry was for love.

Glancing over at Hunter, she couldn't help but think that he had all the qualities she'd ever dreamed of in a husband. He was kind, considerate and, above all, caring. Very few men would have cared enough about an unwed mother keeping her baby to give up their freedom indefinitely.

Sighing, she stared out the windshield of the truck. She wasn't sure what lay ahead of them once they returned to Devil's Fork or how long they'd be husband and wife. But there wasn't a doubt in her mind that no matter what happened, she could count on Hunter being right there beside her to face whatever Craig Culbertson tried to do.

When Callie and Hunter walked into the Life Medevac dispatch room, Mary Lou and the on-duty crew gave them a standing ovation. "Congratulations!"

Grinning like a Cheshire cat, Mary Lou stepped forward. "We've all talked it over and we're giving you two the night off."

"Yeah, we decided you couldn't have a decent wedding night here at the hangar with all of us hanging around," Corey chimed in. His knowing smile made Callie's cheeks heat with embarrassment.

"I'm taking over for you, Hunter," George said. "And Mark, the Evac III paramedic, is coming in to take over for Callie."

"What about standby?" Hunter asked. "We have to have a crew on call in case we have overlapping runs."

"We've got that covered," Mary Lou said, stepping between them. She slipped her arms through theirs and started walking them toward the door. "The rest of the guys are going to take care of that. Now I think you should go back to Callie's place and spend the rest of the night having a little honeymoon fun."

Callie felt as if the heat in her cheeks would burst into flames at any moment. She might have known that Mary Lou would cut to the chase and tell them exactly how she thought they should be spending the evening.

"Hunter?" She felt bad about everyone giving up their day off to cover for them. The least he could do was put up a token protest.

But his sexy grin sent a streak of heat thrumming through her veins and spoke volumes of what an excellent idea he thought the Life Medevac staff had come up with. "Sounds good to me," he said, nodding. He took her hand in his and led her through the door, then, turning back, added, "We'll be back at eight tomorrow morning to finish out our shift."

When they walked into her house several minutes later, Callie took a deep breath and turned to face Hunter. "I don't feel right about this."

He frowned as he reached to take her into his arms. "We're married, darlin'. Making love is something husbands and wives do."

She shook her head and tried to remember what she'd been about to say. With him holding her close, it seemed to short-circuit her thought process. "I was talking about our coworkers giving up their day off."

"Why?" He bent his head to nibble at the sensitive skin along the column of her neck. "I thought it was a nice gesture."

"It…is." A shiver of excitement slid up her spine when he kissed his way to the wildly fluttering pulse at the base of her throat. "But they have no idea…that we aren't making…a lifetime commitment."

Raising his head, he held her gaze with his as he cupped her cheek with his large palm. "Don't worry about it, Callie. We're committed to each other now and for as long as it takes to make sure Culbertson never bothers you again."

"But—"

"Giving us the night off was something they wanted to do, and they know we'll do the same thing for them when they need time off."

His deep, smooth voice and the look in his dark green eyes quickly had her forgetting her guilt or the reason for it. The feel of his hands sliding the length of her back sent shivers of delight coursing through her, and it suddenly didn't matter why they'd gotten married or that it wasn't forever. God help her, but she wanted to spend the night in Hunter's arms again, wanted to feel his hands on her and the sense of being cherished as he made their bodies one.

She would have told him, but when his mouth settled over hers, the contact was so tender it caused tears to flood her eyes and robbed her of the ability to speak. He deepened the kiss, and as his tongue stroked hers, the mating was filled with promises of things to come. He wanted her and he was letting her know in no uncertain terms how much.

When he swung her up into his arms and walked into the bedroom, their lips never broke contact, and as he gently lowered them both to the bed, Callie's heart skipped several beats. With his legs tangling with hers, the strength of his arousal pressed against her thigh and had her own body responding with wanton pulses of need.

His lips clung to hers a moment before he raised his head to smile down at her. "I want you so damned much I can taste it."

"And I want you just as much." Her body tingled with such need she trembled from it. "Please, make love to me, Hunter."

His slumberous look thrilled her to the depths of her soul as he rose from the bed to remove their shoes and socks, then, taking her by the hand, he pulled her to her feet. Bringing her hands to rest on his chest, he gave her a smile that caused her knees to wobble.

"Let's do this together, darlin'."

Excited by the prospect of removing his clothes, Callie rose up on tiptoes to kiss the skin just above the neck band of his red T-shirt at the same time she tugged the tail of it from the waistband of his jeans. Sliding her hands under the soft cotton garment, she felt his muscles contract as she slowly pushed the shirt up along his lean sides. When he raised his arms to help her, she allowed him to pull the garment over his head and toss it aside.

"Your body is perfect," she said, lightly running her fingertips over his well-defined pectoral muscles.

When she traced circles around his flat male nipples, he sucked in a sharp breath. "As good as having your hands on my chest feels, it's my turn."

Reaching for her, he gently pulled the blue scrunchie holding her ponytail free and threaded his fingers through the shoulder-length strands. "Your hair is like fine threads of golden silk."

He tilted her head for a quick kiss, then with painstaking care worked the three buttons at the top of her oversize polo shirt through the buttonholes. Slowly, carefully lifting it up and over her head, his gaze held hers captive as he reached behind her to unfasten her bra. By the time he slid the silk and lace from her shoulders to toss it on top of their shirts, their breathing sounded as if they'd both run a marathon.

The look in his eyes warmed her all over as he filled both of his hands with her breasts and chafed the sensitive tips to harden peaks with his thumbs. "You're so beautiful, Callie."

He dipped his head to capture one of her nipples with his mouth, and she had to brace her hands on his shoulders to keep from melting into a puddle at his feet.

He teased first one, then the other tight nub with his tongue, and it felt as if her blood turned to warm honey as tendrils of desire threaded their way through her limbs to pool with an aching emptiness between her thighs. When he finally raised his head, the hungry look in his dark green eyes stole her breath.

Without a word, she reached for his belt and quickly worked the leather through the metal buckle. But when she popped the snap at the top of his jeans, she forced herself to slow down. Glancing up at him, she smiled as she traced her fingernail along each metal tooth of his bulging zipper. "This looks a bit uncomfortable. I think you'd probably feel better if we got you out of these."

"I don't *think,* darlin', I *know* I'd feel better," he said, his voice sounding raspy.

Easing his fly open, she pushed the jeans down his lean hips, then past his muscular thighs and calves. When he stepped out of them, she trailed her hands along his hair-roughened skin on her way back up to his navy-blue boxer briefs. She loved the way the sinew flexed and bunched at her touch.

"Is that better now?"

His sexy grin sent heat spiraling straight to her core. "Oh, yeah," he said, reaching for the waistband of her maternity jeans.

His heated gaze held hers captive as he slid his fingers under the elastic. His warm palms felt wonderful brushing against her skin as he knelt to push the jeans down her legs, then slowly skimmed his hands along her legs on his way back to her silk panties. Touching her between her legs, he applied a light pressure against the most sensitive spot on her body, sending waves of pleasure radiating through her.

"Does that feel good, Callie?" he asked when a tiny moan of pleasure escaped her.

Unable to form a coherent thought, all she could do was nod.

When he stood up, his gaze captured hers, and as if by unspoken agreement they both reached for the last barriers separating them. Never losing eye contact, together they disposed of his boxer briefs and her panties.

Callie's eyes widened at the sight of his magnificent body. When they'd made love the other morning there hadn't been enough light for her to see his physique. But as she gazed at him now, she marveled at how perfectly made he was.

His wide shoulders, chest and thighs were well defined by muscles that she somehow knew hadn't been honed by working out at a gym. As her gaze drifted lower, past his lean flanks, her breath caught at the sight of his proud, full erection. He was impressively built, thoroughly aroused and, as she lifted her eyes to meet his, looking at her as if he thought she was the most beautiful creature on earth.

"You're amazing," he said, his voice thick with passion.

"I was thinking the same thing about you." She might have felt a bit unsure about her expanding shape had it not been for the gleam of appreciation in his eyes and the reverence she detected in his voice.

Reaching out, she tentatively touched him. Shivers of hot, hungry desire streaked through her when she circled him with her hand and his warm, thick strength surged at her touch. Measuring his length and the softness below, she glanced up at him when a groan rumbled up from deep in his chest. His eyes were closed and a muscle ticked along his jaw as if he'd clenched his teeth against the intense sensations her touch created.

"Does that feel good, Hunter?"

When he opened his eyes, the feral light in the green depths caused her to shiver with a need stronger than anything she'd ever experienced before. But when he cupped her breasts, then lowered his head to circle each nipple in turn with his tongue, swirls of heat coursed through her and she abandoned her exploration to place her hands on his shoulders for support.

"P-please…"

"What do you want, Callie?" His warm breath on her sensitized skin made her feel as if she'd go up in flames at any moment.

"You."

"When?"

"Now!" He was driving her crazy and he wanted to play twenty questions?

Chuckling, he raised his head and, wrapping his arms around her, pulled her to him. The instant soft female skin met hard masculine flesh, Callie moaned with pleasure.

"Let's get in bed while we still have the strength," he said hoarsely.

When he helped her into bed, then stretched out beside her, waves of sheer delight danced over every cell in her being at the feel of his calloused palms caressing her ribs and the underside of her breasts. Feeling as if she were burning up from the inside out, she pressed her legs together in an effort to ease the empty ache he'd created there. He must have realized what she needed because he reached down to gently cup her, a moment before his fingers parted her to stroke the tiny nub of hidden pleasure. Waves of heat streaked through her and she felt as if she'd go mad from wanting.

Raining kisses along her collarbone, then up the side of her neck, he moved his finger deeper to stroke her inside. "Is this where you want me, Callie?"

"Y-yes."

"Do you want me there now?"

"Hunter…please—"

"Just a little bit more, darlin'," he said as his relentless fingers continued to stroke her inner core.

"I can't…stand anymore."

When he moved his hand away, he immediately nudged her thighs farther apart with his knee and eased himself into position. He covered her lips with his, and Callie closed her eyes at the exquisite feel of his blunt tip against her a moment before she felt him slowly, surely slip inside.

"Look at me, Callie."

When she opened her eyes, his heated gaze held hers as he set an easy pace, and all too soon she felt her body straining for sweet liberation from the tension he'd created within her. He must have noticed her tightening around him because he steadily increased his thrusts until the coil of need within her snapped and she was cast into the realm of intense pleasure. She heard him call her name at the same time his big body stiffened, then quivered inside of her as he found his own release.

Wrapping her arms around Hunter's broad back, she held him close as her body pulsed with sweet satisfaction. When their bodies began to cool, she bit her lower lip to keep from crying. She'd done the unthinkable. She'd fought against it from the moment they'd met, but there was no sense denying it any longer.

She'd fallen in love with Hunter O'Banyon.

Nine

The next morning, when Hunter and Callie walked into the dispatch room, Mary Lou pointed to a slip of paper on her desk. "Hunter, you have a message from someone by the last name of Barringer." She shook her head disapprovingly. "He wouldn't tell me what the nature of his business was. But he said it was important that you call him as soon as possible." She pointed to a huge box over in the corner. "And the new flight suits you ordered were delivered yesterday afternoon."

"Good," Callie said, walking over to gaze into the box. "I can barely zip the one I have now."

Recognizing the name of the private investigator

he'd hired, Hunter nodded. "While I return his phone call, why don't you and Callie sort through the new flight suits and match them against the list of everyone's sizes." He walked over to kiss Callie's cheek. "I'll be back in a few minutes to help."

Her cheeks colored a deep rose and he didn't think he'd ever seen her look prettier. "Mary Lou and I can handle this. Go make your phone call."

"I can sure tell the two of you are newlyweds," Mary Lou said, laughing. "If you can't be away from her long enough to make a phone call, you've got it bad."

Hunter had no idea why, but he couldn't seem to stop smiling as he picked up the slip of paper with Barringer's number on it and walked down the hall toward his office. Maybe it was because the investigator was reporting back so quickly. But he had a feeling that it had more to do with the fact that he'd just spent the most incredible night of his life with his amazing wife.

Callie was the most responsive, sensual woman he'd ever met, and he couldn't wait for the end of the day when their shift ended and they could get back to her place. Unless they were called out for a standby run, they had four days to resume their honeymoon and he had every intention of making the most of their time off. His body tightened at the thought and he cursed the fact that they had eight hours before they were off duty.

When he closed the office door behind him, he took several deep breaths to calm his runaway libido, then walked over to the desk and dialed Barringer's number. He'd no sooner given his name to the man's secretary than Joe Barringer came on the line.

"I've discovered several things about Culbertson that I think you'll find very interesting," he said without preamble.

"You've got my attention," Hunter said, sinking into the desk chair.

"Craig Culbertson is broke. He's gambled away the trust fund his grandfather left him and it appears that he's started siphoning money out of the one set aside for his son."

"But aren't his parents in control of that money?" Hunter asked. He could've sworn that Callie told him the Culbertsons had adopted Craig's son and raised the boy as their own.

"They were," Barringer said. "But there was a stipulation in his grandfather's will that when Craig reached the age of thirty, he gained control of that fund, as well."

"Anything else?" Hunter asked, wondering how he could use the information to help Callie. So far, he hadn't heard anything worthwhile.

"Yes. It appears that provisions have been made for future children."

Hunter sat up straight in his chair. He had a feeling

he was about to learn the motive behind Culbertson's visit to Devil's Fork. "What kind of provisions?"

"Just a second." It sounded as if Barringer was shuffling papers a moment before he added, "Any future offspring of Craig Culbertson will have a million-dollar trust fund set up and—"

"Let me guess," Hunter said. "Culbertson is the administrator."

"You got it." The disgust in Joe Barringer's voice was evident. "His grandfather must have expected Culbertson to sow more wild oats. Instead of leaving him the lion's share of his estate, the old man stipulated that the majority of his money would be held in trust for future heirs." He paused as if consulting his notes. "And Culbertson has to have custody of each child before a trust will be set up in his or her name."

"That explains a lot," Hunter said, thinking aloud.

"Something else you might find interesting—Culbertson has some pretty shady characters breathing down his neck for past gambling debts. I'm not sure he can wait for Ms. Marshall to give birth. He needs the money now," Barringer finished.

"What about his parents? Can't he go to them for the money?" To Hunter, that would be the obvious choice if the man was in that kind of trouble.

"Harry and Alice Culbertson have pretty much washed their hands of their son," Barringer said. "They've bailed him out several times, and from what I can gather, they put their foot down the last time and told him that was it. They wouldn't pay off any more gambling debts."

"In other words, he's desperate for cash and if he can stall his bookies until Callie has her baby, he'll have one more trust fund to steal from," Hunter said, shaking his head at the man's foolishness.

"That's about it. If I find out anything else, I'll give you a call," Barringer added. "But I think you have the most relevant information now."

When Hunter ended the connection, he immediately called the bank, Luther Freemont, Emerald's assistant, then the bed-and-breakfast where Craig Culbertson was staying. Satisfied that he had everything under control, as soon as the fax came in from Emerald Inc. headquarters, he left the office and walked back into the dispatch room.

"I have some business I need to take care of," he said, putting his arms around Callie. "When I get back from town, there's something I need to tell you."

Concern lined her forehead. "It sounds serious."

"Nothing for you to be worried about, darlin'." Not caring that Corey and Mary Lou were avid spectators, he gave her a quick kiss. "I'll be back as soon as I can."

"If we need you, we'll page you," Mary Lou said, pouring herself a cup of her god-awful coffee.

As Hunter drove into Devil's Fork, he couldn't wait to confront Culbertson. He was about to make the man an offer Culbertson couldn't afford to turn down. And within the next couple of hours Hunter fully expected for Craig Culbertson to be headed back to Houston and out of Callie's life for good.

"I have to admit, your demand that we have this meeting came as a bit of a surprise, O'Banyon."

Seated in a booth at the back of the Longhorn Café, Hunter stared across the table at the most despicable human being he'd ever had the displeasure to meet. With his slick good looks, sophisticated air and boyish smile, Hunter could understand why women would find Craig Culbertson attractive.

But Hunter knew the type. Guys like Culbertson used their assets to hide their true nature, and Hunter never thought he'd ever admit it, but the man seated across from him was even lower than Owen Larson. As irresponsible as Owen had been about impregnating women, then leaving them to face single motherhood alone, he'd never used his offspring as pawns to bail himself out of a jam.

"I'm going to make you a one-time offer, Culbertson. And if you're as smart as you try to lead people to believe, you'll take it."

"Oh, really?" The man's sneering expression made Hunter want to reach across the table and grab him by the throat.

"I'm going to write you a check for five hundred

thousand dollars, then you're going to sign a document relinquishing all rights to Callie's baby." Hunter knew the moment he mentioned the money that he had the man's attention. "You'll leave town and never bother Callie or her child again."

"What makes you think I can be bought off that easily?" Culbertson asked, not even bothering to sound offended by Hunter's demands. "And who's to say that once I sign that paper, I won't discover that your check is no good?"

"Believe me, the check is good." Leaning forward, Hunter lowered his voice to a menacing growl. "And I happen to know that if you don't get your hands on some money, and damned quick, your life won't be worth spit."

Culbertson paled visibly. "What makes you say that?"

"It's amazing what a good P.I. can uncover, like the bookies coming after you for your gambling debts." Hunter removed the fax he'd received from Emerald Inc.'s legal department from one of his pockets and shoved it across the table. "This is a confidentiality and custody agreement. Sign it, accept my check and clear out of town or run the risk of not only losing the trust fund that would be set up for Callie's baby but your life, as well."

"Is that a threat, O'Banyon?"

Hunter shook his head. "Not at all. Although I'd like

to take you apart limb by limb, I won't have to do a damned thing. Your bookies will take care of that for me." He held up his hand to get the waitress's attention. "I'm going to order a cup of coffee. By the time I'm finished with it, you'd better have signed that document or the offer is rescinded and you can take your chances with the bookies and the court system."

After the waitress brought Hunter's coffee, Culbertson gave him a cocky grin. "Why should I settle for half a million? If I wanted to, I could get custody of Callie's brat in a heartbeat and end up with a full million at my disposal."

"I wouldn't count on that." Hunter gave the man a confident smile. "For one thing, Callie and I really are husband and wife. That will go a long way in her favor."

"Oh, that's rich," Culbertson laughed. "You own a run-down air-ambulance service in Nowheresville that I'm sure barely makes ends meet and you expect me to believe that my lawyers and good friend Judge Howell would rather see a child raised by you and Callie than in the lifestyle I could provide."

Hunter took a sip of the coffee, then slowly set his cup back on the saucer. "You don't get it, do you, Culbertson?"

"What's to get? I can tie this up in court for years and I know for certain Callie doesn't have that kind of money." His expression condescending, he shook his head. "And I seriously doubt that you do either."

"You might be surprised who could tie who up in court." Hunter laughed harshly. "Besides, I doubt that your bookies would want to wait that long before they start taking their money out of your worthless hide."

Hunter could tell that he'd given Culbertson something to think about. But the man was more arrogant and self-absorbed than Hunter had given him credit for.

"What if I say half a mil isn't enough? What if I want more?"

"It's up to you." Hunter took a healthy swallow of his coffee. "But I'm getting close to finishing this coffee. If you haven't signed that paper by the time I get done, Callie and I will see you in court." He grinned. "That is, if there's anything left of you by the time the case comes up on the docket."

When Hunter started to pick up his cup, he watched Culbertson glance at the contents, then eye the document in front of him. "And you're sure the check is good?"

Hunter nodded. "I can guarantee it."

"How do I know I can trust you?"

"That's something you'll just have to take on faith," Hunter said, lifting his cup. He almost laughed out loud when Culbertson quickly took an ink pen from the inside pocket of his sports jacket and hastily scrawled his name on the designated line of the document before Hunter could take the last sip of the coffee.

Shoving the paper back at him, Culbertson glared at

Hunter as he folded it and put it in his pocket. "You're welcome to Callie and her brat. Now where's my money?"

Hunter removed a check from a zippered pocket on his flight suit, then, before he could stop himself, he reached across the table and grabbed Culbertson by the front of the shirt. Pulling him forward until they were nose to nose, he made sure there was no mistaking the menace in his voice. "Don't ever let me hear you use that tone of voice again when you refer to my wife or our baby. You got that?"

"You really love her, don't you?"

"Yes, I do." When Hunter realized what he'd said, he released Culbertson's shirt and shoved him away. Then, sliding out of the booth, he tossed the check on the table. "Now get the hell out of Devil's Fork and don't let me see you again."

As he walked out of the café and got into his truck, Hunter's heart pounded hard in his chest and he had to force himself to breathe. He loved Callie.

When he'd lost Ellen, he'd vowed never to love another woman and run the risk of losing her. But as much as he'd cared for his fiancée, his feelings for her couldn't compare to the depths of what he felt for Callie. In the past couple of weeks he'd felt more alive than he had in his entire life and he knew for certain that if he lost her he'd never survive.

How the hell had he let himself get in so deep?

When had it happened? And why hadn't he seen it coming?

Somewhere between that wild ride from the airfield when she'd picked him up the day he'd arrived in Devil's Fork and yesterday when they'd exchanged wedding vows he'd let go of the past and reached for the future. A future with Callie and her son.

Steering the truck out onto Main Street, he shook his head. He wasn't fool enough to think that just because he realized he loved her they could work things out and make a go of their marriage. At the time he'd suggested they get married, she'd had just as many reservations, if not more, than he'd had. And the sole reason they'd married in the first place was to keep Culbertson from taking her baby away from her. Now that he was no longer a threat, their reason for staying together was gone.

He took a deep breath as he turned onto the drive leading up to the Life Medevac hangar. He knew that Callie cared for him. Her response to his kisses and the passion they shared when they made love was proof of that. But did she love him?

She'd told him that she trusted him, but that didn't mean she wanted to stay with him for the rest of her life. And he distinctly remembered her telling him the first day they met that she was quite content to remain single.

He also recalled Callie had a problem with anyone

who had money. How would she take it when she discovered that she was married to a man with a multimillion-dollar bank account and who stood to inherit a sizable portion of Emerald Inc., the multibillion-dollar enterprise his paternal grandmother had built from the ground up?

As he parked the truck, got out and walked toward the hangar, he wasn't sure how things would turn out for them. But he had every intention of finding out. He'd tell her how he felt, explain everything about himself and pray that she understood and loved him anyway.

"I was just about to page you," Mary Lou said, hanging up the phone.

"There's been an accident on the Thompson ranch and they need us there as soon as possible," Callie added as she breezed past him on the way out the door.

"Where's Corey?" he asked, following her.

"Right here, boss," Corey called, running after them.

When they were all strapped into their seats, Hunter revved the helicopter's engine and took hold of the stick. He wasn't happy about having to postpone his talk with Callie, but it couldn't be helped. They had an accident victim waiting on them and that took precedence over matters of the heart.

After stabilizing the compound fracture on Carl Thompson's leg and transporting him to the hospital in El Paso, Callie was more than ready to get back to base. It had taken everything she and Corey could do to convince the man that he wasn't on a joyride and couldn't sit up to look out the window during the thirty-minute flight.

"I hope old Carl isn't overly accident-prone," Corey said as they climbed back into the helicopter.

Callie nodded. "If it had taken much longer to get here, I would have radioed for a doctor's order to give him a sedative."

"Well, that's something you won't have to give me," Corey said, taking off his headset and settling back in his seat. "I intend to catch a few winks on the flight home."

When Corey closed his eyes and fell silent, Callie turned her attention to Hunter. As she watched, he put on his headset and flipped switches on the control panel. Her heart skipped a beat and she had to remind herself to breathe. If she lived to be a hundred, she didn't think she'd ever see a man look as sexy as he looked in his flight suit and aviator sunglasses. But then, she thought he was sexy no matter what he did or didn't wear.

She took a deep breath. As hard as she'd fought to keep from loving him, he'd managed to get past her defenses and fill a void in her life that she hadn't even known existed.

Unfortunately that didn't mean they could have a future together. He'd made it quite clear that he was only marrying her to help her retain custody of her son and that once the threat from Craig was over, so was their marriage. Besides, pretending to be happily married and anticipating the birth of a child was one thing. Permanently accepting the role of loving husband and expectant father was something else entirely.

Her chest tightened as she thought of her life without Hunter. She didn't want to think about not being able to see his handsome face every day, hear his hearty laughter or feel the warmth of his touch. But did she have the nerve to tell him how she felt and that she wanted to stay married after her current problems were resolved?

"Damn!" Hunter's vehement curse coming through her headset broke through her disturbing introspection.

"What's wrong?"

"We've got some weather moving in that I don't like," he said, pointing to a bank of clouds.

As she listened to him radio for a weather report from the control tower at the El Paso airport, she was relieved to hear the storm front was moving away from them. She'd never been overly frightened by heavy turbulence in an airplane, but she wasn't sure she wanted to experience it in a helicopter.

"Looks like we're in the clear," he said, lifting off the helipad and steering the helicopter back toward Devil's Fork.

"Did you get your business taken care of this morning?" she asked conversationally.

He nodded. "When we get back to base, we have some things we need to discuss."

"That sounds rather ominous." She wasn't sure from the serious tone of his voice that she wanted to hear what he had to say.

"Don't worry, darlin'. It's not as bad as it sounds."

His endearment reassured her, and they flew in companionable silence for some time before Hunter rattled off a string of blistering curses, ending with a word that most men saved for extreme circumstances.

"I'm almost afraid to ask, but what was that for?" she asked.

"The winds have shifted and we're about to fly right into the middle of that weather front," he said as a gust of wind buffeted the helicopter.

As Hunter fought the stick, Callie tightened her shoulder harness and did her best not to scream when they swayed precariously. Praying they were close to the Life Medevac base, her heart sank when she glanced out the side window and saw the jagged peaks of the mountains.

"I hope like hell I can find a place to set down," Hunter said as he continued to struggle with the controls. "We need to ride this out on the ground."

"That sounds like a good idea to me," she readily agreed.

Glancing over at Corey, she couldn't believe he was still asleep. No wonder Mary Lou complained about trying to wake him up when their crew had a night run to make.

"This is going to be risky," Hunter said, sounding as if his teeth were clenched. "I want you and Corey to hang on tight."

She gripped the sides of the jump seat. "I don't know how, but Corey is still asleep."

"Does he have the shoulder harness buckled?"

"Yes. But he disconnected his headset."

"That's okay," Hunter said tersely. "All that matters is that he's strapped in."

Callie felt as if her heart was in her throat. She knew enough about helicopters to know that landing in a mountainous area was tricky under the best conditions. But during a storm with strong wind gusts it was going to be extremely hazardous.

She felt the helicopter suddenly lurch to one side, and closing her eyes, she prayed as hard as she could while she waited for whatever happened next.

When Hunter spotted a relatively level area at the base of one of the mountains, he clenched his teeth and used every ounce of strength he had to hold the chopper as steady as possible. Fleeting images of another emergency landing and the devastating outcome flashed through his mind. But this time would be different. He was determined that this time the woman he loved and her unborn child would be safe and unharmed.

When the skids bumped the ground hard, then bounced up to come down again with a bone-jarring thud, Hunter killed the rotor engine and released the latch on his shoulder harness. Saying a silent prayer of thanks to the powers that be for a safe, albeit rough, landing, he climbed into the cabin area to check on his passengers.

Taking Callie into his arms, he held her close. "Are you all right?"

She clung to him as she nodded. "Y-yes."

Turning to Corey, Hunter asked, "What about you? Are you okay?"

Pale as a ghost, his eyes wide with shock, the young man nodded. "Wow! That was one hairy landing. Where are we?"

Hunter looked out the starboard windows at the surrounding mountains. "About halfway between El Paso and Devil's Fork."

The adrenaline high he'd been on since realizing they were on a collision course with the storm began to wane, and Hunter felt as if his muscles had turned to jelly. Reaching for the microphone clipped to the epaulet on Callie's flight suit, he radioed Mary Lou to advise her of the situation. Then, after assuring her they were all okay, he told her they would start back as soon as the storm let up.

Unable to stop thinking about how close he'd come to reliving the nightmare he'd been caught up in five years ago and not wanting Callie to see that his hands were beginning to shake, he made up a lame excuse about doing a systems check and climbed back into the pilot's seat.

He was vaguely aware that Callie and Corey were discussing Corey's sleeping habits, but Hunter paid little attention to the conversation. He was too busy thinking about what could have happened if he'd been unable to land the chopper safely.

What would he have done if he'd lost Callie the way he'd lost Ellen? How could he have lived with himself?

He took a deep breath, then slowly released it. The answer was simple. He couldn't. And with sudden insight he knew exactly what he had to do.

As soon as they returned to the hangar, he'd hand Callie the document Culbertson had signed, tell her she was free to pursue an annulment, then terminate her employment at Life Medevac.

Ten

By the time she, Hunter and Corey returned to the hangar, it was time for their shift to end, and Callie was more than ready to turn over the watch to the Evac II crew and go home. Her nerves were still jangled from narrowly escaping a crash landing and she needed to talk to Hunter. He hadn't said more than a handful of words since the incident, and she could tell something was bothering him.

Well, that made two of them. While they'd waited out the storm, Corey had chattered about everything from being hard to wake up to his pregnant girlfriend and their impending wedding, but Callie hadn't paid much attention. She'd been too preoccupied with thoughts of her baby and how close she'd come to losing him.

"I've got a couple of things to take care of here at the office," Hunter said, walking up behind her. "If you don't mind, I'll be over a little later."

Turning to face him, her smile faded at his serious expression. "Is there a problem?"

He hesitated before shaking his head. "No. I'm just not looking forward to the paperwork I have to do."

"We left my car here last night and I need to get it home anyway. I'll see you in an hour or so." When he gave her a short nod and started to turn to walk back down the hall to his office, she asked, "What would you like for dinner?"

"Don't worry about anything for me. I'm not hungry." Then without another word he disappeared down the hall.

She'd only known him for a couple of weeks, but that didn't matter. There was no doubt in her mind that something was terribly wrong, and she had every intention of finding out what it was.

But a hangar full of people wasn't the best place to have a heart-to-heart talk with her husband, and Callie decided that biding her time would be her best option. When Hunter came over, she'd find out what was bothering him, then tell him her news. She was going to grant his wish and ground herself, at least until after her son was born. And, unless she changed her mind, there was the strong possibility that she might give up being a flight nurse permanently.

As she drove the short distance to her house, she placed her hand on her rounded stomach. She knew it would take Hunter some time to find a replacement for her, but that couldn't be helped. Effective immediately, she was resigning her position at Life Medevac to concentrate on becoming a mother and being there for her son as he grew up.

Parking his truck in Callie's driveway, Hunter sat for several minutes staring at her little house. In the past couple of weeks he'd been happier visiting the cozy little cottage than he'd been in five long years, and it was tearing him apart to think that after tonight he would no longer be welcome there.

But what he was about to do was best for all concerned and he knew that Callie would eventually understand that. And even if she didn't, he could at least sleep at night knowing that he'd done everything in his power to protect her and the baby.

When he got out of the truck, he gripped the folder with the papers he was about to give her and slowly climbed the steps to knock on the door. As soon as he got this over with, he had every intention of driving out to that spot he'd found a few days after he'd arrived in Devil's Fork where he could stare at the stars. Maybe if he stayed there long enough, he'd come to terms with the fact that to protect the woman and child he loved with all his heart, he had to give them up.

"Why did you knock?" Callie asked when she opened the door and stood back for him to enter. "Why didn't you just come on in?"

Standing there with her silky blond hair down around her shoulders, flour streaked across her blue maternity top and the prettiest smile he'd ever seen, she was causing his heart to twist painfully in his chest and she didn't even know it.

Walking past her into the living room, Hunter waited until she closed the door, then turned to face her. "We have to talk."

Her smile faded. "Does this have something to do with what happened this afternoon? Because if it does—"

"We were damned lucky this afternoon," he said, cutting her off. He hadn't meant to sound so harsh, but it was taking every ounce of strength he had not to take her in his arms and abandon the course of action he knew he had to take.

"Hunter?"

She extended her hand and took a step toward him, but, shaking his head, he moved away. He knew beyond a shadow of doubt that if she touched him, he'd lose his internal battle. And it was one he knew that he had to win.

"I think you'd better sit down for this," he said, tempering the tone of his voice.

Sinking onto the love seat, she stared up at him with troubled eyes. "You're beginning to frighten me."

"I don't mean to." He took a deep breath and opened the folder in his hand to remove the document that Culbertson had signed earlier in the day. Handing it to her, he explained what he'd learned from the private investigator and about his meeting with Culbertson. "You won't be hearing any more from Craig Culbertson. He's gone back to Houston and won't bother you or your son again."

She gave him a disbelieving look. "You paid him off?"

Hunter shrugged. "I guess you could call it that."

"My God, I can't allow you to do that. That's an exorbitant amount of money."

"Too late, darlin'. It's already done."

Staring at the paper for several seconds, when she looked up at him, she shook her head. "You can't afford this and I can't possibly pay you back."

"I'm not asking you to," he said firmly. "Consider it a baby gift."

"A baby gift is a set of bibs or a high chair. It's certainly not as extravagant as half a million dollars to get someone to leave me alone."

"Don't worry about it. I'm not."

"Hunter, please—"

When she started to rise from the love seat, he shook his head. "I'm not finished yet. Now that the threat from Culbertson is over with, you're free to petition the courts for an annulment."

She sucked in a sharp breath. "Is that what you want?"

It was the last thing he wanted, but he couldn't tell her that. "I believe that was our agreement."

Standing up, she walked over to him. "You didn't answer my question."

"It doesn't matter what I want." He handed her the folder. "After you take a look at this, I'm sure you'll agree that an annulment is for the best."

When she scanned the termination of employment papers he'd drafted and the severance check for a year's wages, she glared at him. "Why am I being fired? And why are you giving me so much money?"

"Because it's the only way I can think of to keep you from flying. There's enough money that you should be able to pay for the birth, as well as stay home with your son for several months." He'd known she wouldn't be happy about it, but that couldn't be helped. It was for her own good and his peace of mind.

"This won't keep me from flying," she said, tossing it onto the coffee table. "I'm an experienced flight nurse. If I wanted to, I could get a job with another air-ambulance service. But I've decided—"

"You'd better not." Before he could stop himself, he reached out to take her by the upper arms. "What happened today was just a glimpse of what could happen every time you climb into a helicopter to make an emergency run. Promise me you'll find a job in a hospital somewhere."

"Hunter, why…are you…doing this to me?" she asked haltingly.

He closed his eyes for a moment, and when he opened them, the tears on her porcelain cheeks caused a pain to knife through him that threatened to knock him to his knees. He didn't like talking about the accident, but he had to make her understand why he couldn't bear the thought of her flying.

"Five years ago I was behind the controls of a helicopter that went down in Central America. It was a mechanical problem and there wasn't a damn thing I could do to stop the crash from happening. I lost my fiancée and our unborn child that day." Wrapping his arms around Callie, he pulled her to him. "I can't and won't let that happen to you."

"That's why you've wanted me to ground myself from the day you got here."

Unable to get words past the cotton lining his throat, he nodded.

Leaning back, she looked up at him. "Why, Hunter? Why can't you let that happen again?"

"Because I love you, dammit." Realizing what he'd said, he immediately released her, stepped back and, reaching up, rubbed the tension gathering at the back of his neck. "Whenever you get ready, stop by the hangar and clean out your locker."

"Are you finished saying what you came here to tell me?"

Fully expecting her to demand that he leave, he started for the door. "Yes."

"Good." She walked up to him and stabbed her finger at his chest. "Now you're going to listen to me."

"I won't change my mind."

Her violet eyes sparkled with anger. "I don't care. You've had your say and I'm going to have mine."

He guessed it was only fair, but it didn't make standing there wanting to hold her and knowing he couldn't any easier. "All right. Make it quick."

"Number one, I'll take as long as I want to tell you what I think. And number two, you need to stop being so bossy and learn to listen." She waved one delicate hand toward the door. "From the minute you walked in here I've been trying to tell you something and you wouldn't let me get a word in edgewise."

"I can't see that it will make a difference."

She folded her arms beneath her breasts and tapped her bare foot against the floor. "Why don't you sit down and hear me out before you start making judgments."

He shook his head. "I don't think—"

"Sit!"

Lowering himself into the armchair, he gazed up at

her. She was working up a full head of steam and he didn't think he'd ever seen her look more beautiful. But then, when a man loved a woman the way he loved Callie, there was never a time when she didn't look beautiful to him.

"If you had let me talk earlier, I could have spared us both a lot of anguish." Standing in front of him, she propped her hands on her hips. "I was going to tell you that after what happened today, I realized that I no longer want to be a flight nurse. So you can take that termination notice and your severance check and stick them where the sun doesn't shine."

Suddenly feeling as if a heavy weight had been lifted from his shoulders, he sat up a little straighter in the chair. "You don't want to fly anymore?"

"No, I don't." She placed her hand on her stomach. "What happened today reminded me of what's important."

Hunter couldn't believe the degree of relief coursing through him. "You have no idea how glad I am to hear you say that."

"And something else." She began to pace. "What gives you the right to tell me what I should do about our marriage? Did it ever occur to you that I might not want an annulment?"

He couldn't believe that she might want the same thing he did—to try to make their marriage work. Almost afraid to hope, he asked cautiously, "You don't?"

"No. An annulment is the last thing I want." She shook her head. "Although, at the moment I'm questioning my sanity and the reason why I love you, you big lug."

Hunter couldn't have stayed in that chair if his life depended on it. Jumping to his feet, he took her into his arms and held her close.

"Thank God!" Giving her a kiss that left them both gasping for breath, when he raised his head, he felt as if his soul had been set free at the love he saw shining in her pretty eyes. "I want to live the rest of my life with you, darlin'." He placed his palm over her rounded stomach. "And if you're agreeable, I'd like to be a father to your baby."

"I'd like that very much." Tears filled Callie's eyes as she reached up to touch his lean cheek. When she'd come to Devil's Fork, she'd had no idea that in running from her past, she'd find her and her son's future. "You're a special man, Hunter O'Banyon."

"I don't know about that, but I promise I'll be the best husband and father I can be," he said, kissing her. "And the first thing I'm going to do for my new family is add a couple of rooms onto the house." He nibbled tiny kisses to the hollow below her ear. "Or, if you'd like, I can build us a new home with lots of bedrooms for babies, as well as guest rooms for grandmothers to visit."

"Could we afford something like that?" Shivering

with desire, she closed her eyes when Hunter cupped her breast to tease her taut nipple through the fabric of her shirt. "You had to spend a lot of money to get rid of Craig."

When his hand stilled, she opened her eyes to look at him. "What?"

"There's something else you don't know about me," he said, looking a bit uncomfortable.

"You mortgaged Life Medevac to pay off Craig," she guessed, hating that he'd put his business in jeopardy for her sake. "Don't worry, I'm a registered professional nurse. After the baby's born, I'll see what jobs are available."

"That won't be ne—"

"I promise I'll make sure the job is on the ground," she hurriedly reassured him.

"But, darlin'—"

"There might be a traveling nurse's position with the tricounty health department. At any rate, I'll be able to help with the loan payments and I can cut a few corners here and—"

His deep chuckle sent a streak of heat straight to her core as he placed his hand over her mouth. "Now which one of us isn't letting the other get a word in edgewise?"

She playfully touched the tip of her tongue to his palm and watched his eyes darken to forest-green. "I love you," she murmured, letting her lips brush his calloused skin.

He shuddered against her a moment before he took his hand away. "I love you, too, Callie." His expression turned serious. "But there's something more I need to tell you about myself."

Her heart stalled at the apprehension she detected in his voice. "What is it?"

"Remember me telling you about not knowing who my father was until just a few months ago and that his family had money?"

She nodded. "That's when you found out you have two brothers and your grandmother's reason for keeping your father's identity a secret."

"Right." His wide chest rose and fell against her breasts as he drew in a deep breath, and she could tell he was reluctant to say more.

"Surely it can't be all that bad."

He shook his head. "Most people wouldn't think so, but you might feel differently."

"Why do you say that?"

"Because you're not overly fond of wealthy people." He gave her a sheepish grin. "Darlin', I'm rich." He shook his head. "Actually I'm not just rich, I'm filthy rich."

"You're what?" Of all the things that had run through her mind, his being wealthy wasn't one of them. He certainly didn't act like any of the wealthy people she knew.

"When my grandmother finally told me and my

brothers who our father was, she also informed us that we each have a multimillion-dollar trust fund and will one day inherit part of a multibillion-dollar enterprise."

Callie's mouth dropped open and she couldn't have strung two words together if her life depended on it. When she finally found her voice, she asked, "Who is your grandmother?"

He smiled. "Emerald Larson."

"*The* Emerald Larson?"

"The one and only," he said nodding. "I hope you won't hold that against me."

She shook her head. "I can't believe…I mean, you never acted any differently than anyone else and I had no idea—"

He silenced her babbling with a kiss, and by the time he raised his head, she couldn't have cared less how much money he had or who his grandmother was. All that mattered was the man she loved more than life itself was holding her securely against him.

"Hunter, I don't care how much money you have or if you have any at all. I love you and that's all that matters."

"And I love you. Never doubt that." His smile heated her from the top of her head all the way to her bare toes. "By the way, what do you have planned for the end of next month?"

"The same thing I have planned for the rest of my life—loving you." He nuzzled the side of her neck, sending shivers of delight skipping over every cell in her body. "Why?"

When she kissed the strong column of his neck, he groaned and swung her up into his arms. "It doesn't matter. Right now I can't think past taking you into the bedroom and getting started on the rest of our lives."

"I like the way you think, flyboy." Circling his wide shoulders with her arms, as he carried her into the bedroom, she whispered close to his ear, "I love you, Hunter."

"And I love you, Callie." Gently lowering her to the bed, he stretched out beside her, then gathered her into his arms. "And I intend to spend the rest of my life showing you just how much."

Epilogue

As Emerald Larson watched her three grandsons and their wives circulate among the guests at the dinner party she'd put together in their honor, she gave herself a mental pat on the back for a job well done. She'd specifically chosen the companies she'd given each of them to run, as well as arranged for them to meet the women she'd known would be perfect for them, and she couldn't have been more pleased with the results of her efforts.

Glancing at her youngest grandson, Caleb, she smiled fondly. He'd proven to be a genius with his innovative and creative approach to management and had not only improved morale at Skerritt and Crowe

Financial Consultants, he'd increased productivity by fifty percent in just a few months. Along with his wife, Alyssa, he was building a solid reputation as a force to contend with in the financial world.

Turning her attention to her middle grandson, she couldn't have been more proud. Upon his return to the Sugar Creek Ranch, Nick had not only reclaimed his birthright, he'd courageously faced his nemesis and found vindication after thirteen long years. With the help of his wife, Cheyenne, Emerald had no doubt that his plans to turn the cattle company into a free-range operation would meet with complete success. And in the spring, when their first child was born, they'd finally realize their dream of raising a family in that big, charming ranch house under the wide Wyoming sky.

When her gaze landed on Hunter, her oldest grandson, Emerald sighed contentedly. He'd been the one she'd worried about the most. After losing his fiancée and their unborn child, he'd given up flying the helicopters he loved and built a wall around his heart that she'd feared might never come down. But when he'd arrived to take over running the Life Medevac Helicopter Service, he'd not only recaptured his love of flying, he'd met Callie, a young expectant mother whose love had helped him let go of the past and healed his wounded heart.

"You wanted to see me, Mrs. Larson?" Luther Freemont asked, walking up beside her.

As a personal assistant, Luther was highly efficient, his loyalty unsurpassed. But as a man, he was the biggest stuffed shirt she'd ever met.

"I want to thank you for helping me accomplish my goal," she said, continuing to watch her grandsons and their wives. "Our efforts have worked quite well, don't you think?"

"I'd say they've been a resounding success," Luther agreed with her.

"I rather enjoyed watching my grandsons prove themselves with the businesses I gave them to run, as well as helping them find the loves of their lives." She sighed. "It's a shame that I don't have more grandchildren."

Her breath caught and her mood lightened considerably when Luther gave her one of his rare smiles. "Well, as a matter of fact…"

* * * * *

Silhouette Desire.

What Happens in Vegas...

Their Million-Dollar Night

by

KATHERINE GARBERA

(SD #1720)

Roxy O'Malley is just the kind of hostess
corporate sophisticate Max Williams needs
for some R & R while at the casinos. Will one
white-hot night lead to a trip to the altar?

**Don't miss the exciting conclusion
to WHAT HAPPENS IN VEGAS...
available this April from
Silhouette Desire.**

On Sale April 2006
Available at your favorite retail outlet.

Silhouette® Desire

COMING NEXT MONTH

#1717 THE FORBIDDEN TWIN—Susan Crosby
The Elliotts
Seducing your twin sister's ex-fiancé by pretending to be her…
not the best idea. Unless he succumbs.

#1718 THE TEXAN'S FORBIDDEN AFFAIR—
Peggy Moreland
A Piece of Texas
He swept her off her feet, then destroyed her. Now he wants her
back!

#1719 EXPECTING LONERGAN'S BABY—
Maureen Child
Summer of Secrets
He was home just for the summer—until a night of explosive
passion gave him a reason to stay.

#1720 THEIR MILLION-DOLLAR NIGHT—
Katherine Garbera
What Happens in Vegas…
This businessman has millions at stake in a deal but one woman
has him risking scandal and damning the consequences!

#1721 BABY, I'M YOURS—Catherine Mann
It was only supposed to be a weekend affair, then an unexpected
pregnancy changed all of the rules.

#1722 THE SOLDIER'S SEDUCTION—
Anne Marie Winston
She thought the man who'd taken her innocence was gone
forever…until he returned home to claim her—and the daughter
he never knew existed.

SDCNM0306